All Hats on Deck

Books by Sandra Bretting

MURDER AT MORNINGSIDE

SOMETHING FOUL AT SWEETWATER

SOMEONE'S MAD AT THE HATTER

DEATH COMES TO DOGWOOD MANOR

ALL HATS ON DECK

Published by Kensington Publishing Corporation

All Hats on Deck

Sandra Bretting

LYRICAL UNDERGROUND
Kensington Publishing Corp.
www.kensingtonbooks.com

LYRICAL UNDERGROUND BOOKS are published by

Kensington Publishing Corp.
119 West 40th Street
New York, NY 10018

All Kensington titles, imprints, and distributed lines are available at special quantity discounts for bulk purchases for sales promotion, premiums, fund-raising, educational, or institutional use.

Special book excerpts or customized printings can also be created to fit specific needs. For details, write or phone the office of the Kensington Sales Manager: Kensington Publishing Corp., 119 West 40th Street, New York, NY 10018. Attn. Sales Department. Phone: 1-800-221-2647.

Lyrical Underground and Lyrical Underground logo Reg. US Pat. & TM Off.

First Electronic Edition: September 2019
ISBN-13: 978-1-5161-0578-6 (ebook)
ISBN-10: 1-5161-0578-8 (ebook)

First Print Edition: September 2019
ISBN-13: 978-1-5161-0575-5
ISBN-10: 1-5161-0575-3

Printed in the United States of America

Chapter 1

The stand of cedars parted naturally up ahead, their ridged trunks half-submerged in the river, while their branches soared skyward to create a leafy canopy overhead.

We glided along the Atchafalaya in our pirogue, the *wwwhhhiiirrr* of the Honda outboard motor only occasionally broken by a spoonbill's cry.

"Look at that one!" I pointed to a particularly large bird we'd flushed from the treetops. Pure white feathers covered the spoonbill's torso, but its wings wore pink fringe, thanks to the bird's steady diet of grass shrimp. It looked like a small flamingo had wandered away from its home in Florida and somehow landed on a bayou in southern Louisiana.

Beatrice smiled and returned her attention to the tiller. My assistant and I had come to this enchanted place to find a certain mobile home nestled on the riverbank here. The owner, Ruby Oubre, was known far and wide for crafting magick potions on a rusted Kenmore stovetop she kept in the tumbledown home.

But it wasn't her voodoo skills that summoned us out today; it was a favor I owed the old woman.

A few months ago, one of my best friends, Detective Lance LaPorte, discovered a body out here on the bayou. At first, I thought it was Ruby, so I dashed to the river basin all willy-nilly, only to find her safe and sound and right in the middle of mixing a complicated potion for hexing one's enemies.

Ruby lost track of her ingredients when I arrived and ended up two spoonfuls shy of comfrey root, which ruined the entire batch, so I agreed to make it up to her. The elderly Cajun came to collect on the debt last night when she showed up at my hat studio unannounced.

"*Bon ami*," she'd greeted me, as she stepped through the front door of Crowning Glory. "Ya gone make good on dat favor?"

"My what?" I'd innocently replied, since I'd forgotten all about my earlier faux pas.

"Ya offered up da *lagniappe.* Ma boy done need some help."

The "small gift" Ruby wanted from me was a business lesson for her grandson, Hollis. The boy lived with her, and he'd decided to open an alligator farm for tourists who come to this part of the river to visit the antebellum homes nearby. Ruby wanted me to teach him the finer points of marketing, budgeting, and whatnot, given my success with the hat studio.

Now, milliners and alligator wranglers have about as much in common as spoonbills and wood ducks, but I agreed anyway. Not only did I owe Ruby that favor, but heaven forbid I should be on the receiving end of one of her hexes.

So here we were, my assistant and I, navigating a pirogue down the Atchafalaya River on this beautiful October morning. Although I normally favored Lilly Pulitzer shifts for work, I decided to dress comfortably in khakis and a teal oxford that complemented my naturally auburn hair.

"We don't have far to go." Beatrice's voice rose above the *wwwhhhiiirrr.* "It's just past that huge stump."

Thank goodness Bea agreed to help me. She offered access to a pirogue, which was a flat-bottom boat designed to ply shallow waters, and reliable directions. I, on the other hand, agreed to compensate her with some hot beignets when we returned to town.

She handled the boat's tiller now, while I scanned the shoreline for signs of life. The homesteads here were few and far between, ever since a lumber company gobbled up most of the land for its old-growth cypress trees. The sale angered a lot of locals, who nursed a deep and abiding mistrust for anyone not born in these parts, so the lumber company wisely agreed to let a few old-timers stay. They even deeded the land over to one or two of the elderly folks as a goodwill gesture.

"There it is." Beatrice pointed to a mobile home limned with mold, which sat off the boat's starboard side.

It was easy to recognize Ruby's place. A large plaster-of-paris grotto, studded with blue-painted river rocks, perched tipsily on a stump beside the mobile home. The baby-blue grotto protected a faded statue of the Virgin Mary, who spread her arms wide to welcome folks to her part of the river.

Beatrice expertly guided the pirogue to a dock nearby. Once she cut the engine, I pulled an oar from under my seat and began to row, timing my strokes to a song that immediately popped into my head.

"Row, Row, Row Your Boat" set a rhythm as I plied the shallow water. By the time *life was but a dream*, we'd arrived at the listing dock.

"Uh-oh." I cut the last stroke short and balanced the paddle on the edge of the boat. "Looks like the welcoming committee's back."

Sure enough, a spotted mongrel waited for us at the end of the dock. Just like last time, Jacques, the dappled mongrel, hid behind a rotted piling, his white-tipped tail splayed sideways. Helping Ruby out was one thing, but sacrificing my ankles to her snarling dog was quite another, so I let the oar lay idle.

"You mean Jacques?" Beatrice sounded surprised, although I had no idea why. "He's not that bad."

"Not that bad? How can you say that?" On my last trip down the river, the self-appointed watchdog nearly tore apart my favorite pair of ballet flats.

"Watch." Beatrice wobbily rose and then she pulled a Glad baggie from the pocket of her blue jeans. *"Bon jour, Jacques. Déjeuner!"* She waved a rawhide bone in the air—what she called the dog's breakfast—as if it was a Coast Guard flag.

The mutt noticed immediately. After sniffing the air, he emerged from his hiding place, his tail whirling around like a propeller that threatened to lift him right off the dock.

"Butter my biscuits." I grudgingly returned the oar to the water. "If that doesn't beat all."

After one more quick stanza of "Row, Row, Row Your Boat," I brought the pirogue alongside the dock and tethered it to a rusted cleat. "How'd you know it'd work?"

"You mean the rawhide? Every dog loves 'em. And I brought a ton of them, so he won't bother us anymore."

"Hallelujah and pass the mustard." I waited for Beatrice to toss out the bone, and then I confidently hopped onto the dock and stepped around the slobbering pooch. Once I reached the front door of the mobile home, after first climbing some rickety steps, I rapped against the mesh screen with my knuckles.

"Ouch!" The screen chafed my skin as I knocked. "I sure hope Ruby's home."

"You mean you didn't call first?" Beatrice waited for me on the ground, since the landing was too small to fit both of us.

"She told me not to bother. Said I should just drop in. Apparently, she and Hollis are always here on Thursday mornings." I prepared to knock again when the door slowly creaked open.

"Hello?" It was a teenager's voice, all raspy and low.

"Yes, hello. Is that you, Hollis?" I waited for the boy to emerge from the house, only nothing moved in the darkness. "Your grandmother asked us to stop by today for a visit. Is she home?"

Finally, Hollis showed himself. He stepped from behind the screen door, wearing a wrinkled T-shirt from a Lynyrd Skynyrd concert and some baggy Nike shorts that reached his knees.

"I dunno." When he yawned, the black T-shirt stretched tight across his chest. "I just got up."

"Hollis…it's almost ten." I threw Beatrice a look. Normally, she and I arrived at work at eight in the morning, if not sooner, and today was no exception. *Typical teenager.* "I'm sorry we woke you, but can we come inside?"

"Sure." He swung open the door and took a few steps back, which allowed me to pass through the entry and make my way to the living room.

Nothing had changed since my last visit. Crosses of all shapes and sizes studded a thin wall that separated the living room from a small kitchen, and old copies of the *Bleu Bayou Impartial Reporter* dusted a flowered couch. The smell of fried onions and cayenne pepper tinged the air, which was a bit much for midmorning.

Beatrice hung back by the door, as if she couldn't quite decide whether to enter or not.

"Okay," she finally said, "I've gotta go. I promised my aunt I'd pay her a visit while I was out here. She's about a mile downstream."

I threw her another look. "Can't you stay a few minutes?"

Hollis obviously wasn't ready for visitors, and it'd be nice to have some company in the meantime.

"I'm sorry, but I promised Auntie. It'd hurt her feelings if I didn't show up. It was nice to see you, Hollis. Tell your grandma I said hey."

With that, she disappeared down the steps, leaving me alone with the groggy teen.

Since there was no point in both of us nodding off in the dark living room, I decided to take matters into my own hands.

"So, Hollis, tell me how you're doing." I brushed the sports section off the couch's armrest and took a seat.

"Fine, I guess." He watched me push the newspaper aside. "I graduated high school with a GED this summer. Hey…is that an engagement ring?"

I couldn't help but smile. "You noticed that, huh? And they say teenagers don't pay attention."

"Well, it's huge." He moved in for a better look. "Kinda hard to miss it."

"I got engaged in August. And you know my fiancé. It's Ambrose. Ambrose Jackson."

"Awesome!"

That perked him up a bit, like I knew it would. He and Ambrose became fast friends a few years back when my fiancé provided some much-needed help during a particularly stressful time in the teen's life.

It all began a few years ago, when someone died at Morningside Plantation, the place where Hollis's grandmother worked. A few of the locals pegged Ruby as the murderer, so Ambrose took Hollis under his wing to protect him from the gossip.

Of course, everything worked out in the end, and now Ambrose could do no wrong in Hollis's eyes.

"I knew you'd be pleased," I said. "And you've had a big time lately too. I'm so proud of you for getting your GED."

"Thanks. I made mostly six hundreds on the test, which was good enough for me to go to college, but I don't wanna go."

"I heard about that. Your grandma said you'd rather open a business, and she asked me to help you out a little."

"So that's why you're here." Recognition sparked behind his eyes. "I wondered why you'd come all the way down the river."

Since he was wide awake now, I decided to take full advantage of the situation. "As a matter of fact, why don't we get to work? We can use the kitchen table over there."

I pointed to a pine picnic table placed inside the small kitchen. Unlike the front room, where shadows lurked in every corner, the kitchen was bright and airy. Hollis led the way and I followed, after I first paused to admire a cat-shaped clock balanced on the old Kenmore stove.

"Yep," I said. "Now's as good a time as any. We'll just have to start our lesson without Ruby."

Hollis pulled out one of the benches by the table, and I scooted onto its end.

"Okay," I said. "Let's start with the basics. Do you know anything about writing a business plan?"

The blank look on his face told me he didn't, so I motioned for a pen and a pad of paper that lay near the stovetop. No need to make the boy feel bad for being a beginner.

"It's okay, Hollis. I'll show you how it's done." Once he passed me the supplies, I began to sketch a bell curve. "First, I'll show you something called the normal distribution curve."

Before long, I'd drawn a passable rendering of a bell, which I used to explain supply and demand. Then, I taught him how to write an executive summary. After watching him struggle for a minute or two, I jumped in to help him, and together we wrote a document any business owner would be proud to call his own.

By the time we came up for air, the paws on the cat clock pointed straight at twelve.

"Holy-schmoley!" I jumped up from the bench. I'd planned to spend an hour with Hollis, not two, and there was no telling who—or what—was waiting for me back at my hat studio. "I'm sorry, Hollis, but I have to go."

His eyes widened when he saw the clock too. "Wow. It's noon already. Thanks for coming out here, Miss DuBois. You really saved my hide."

"Well, I don't know about that. A lot of this information is on the Internet." No need for the teen to think I invented the bell curve. "Check out the Small Business Administration's website. There's lots of good information out there, if you know where to look."

"Yes, ma'am." He walked me out of the kitchen, but he paused by the screen door. "I wonder where Granny went? She's gonna be disappointed she couldn't see you off."

"I'm sure she's okay." To be honest, I'd completely forgotten about Ruby. Once I got to talking about supply and demand, everything else went right out the window.

"But this isn't like her." His face darkened a tad. "She usually lets me know if she's gonna be late."

"I think she would've called you if there was trouble."

"Yeah, but the cell phone reception around here sucks." He tried to shake off his worries with a shrug. "But maybe you're right. Maybe she got tied up somewhere."

"That's it. I'm sure that's it. No need to worry just yet."

The last time I visited Ruby, back when I thought she was a goner, she'd insisted she could handle herself out here on the bayou.

"In fact," I added, "she's probably visiting with one of your neighbors and forgot all about the time."

"You're right. She might've even taken our pirogue down the river."

He pronounced it "pee-row," and it reminded me of something else I'd forgotten. "Oh, shine! Beatrice took off in *our* pirogue a while ago. She's probably waiting for me by the dock."

I hurried past Hollis and stepped through the screen door. Oddly enough, I didn't hear the rumble of the boat's motor as I scrambled down the steps. The only sounds came from a soft breeze that *whoosh*ed through the tupelos overhead and then a faint *flap* from something clear and plastic that bobbled on one of the dock's pilings.

Thankfully, there was no sign of Jacques, the property's self-appointed watchdog, so I took a step toward the dock. The shiny plastic flag on the piling looked like the Glad baggie Beatrice had used earlier. She must've tied it to the dock when she finished doling out the dog's treats.

Call it instinct, or call it intuition, but something about the odd placement of the baggie, not to mention the quietness of the bayou, set my teeth on edge. As if everything and everyone but us had already fled the scene. It didn't seem natural, and it made me wonder what everyone else knew that we didn't.

Chapter 2

I glanced over my shoulder at Hollis as I strode toward the dock. "I wonder where Beatrice went?"

"Too bad you can't just call her," he said. "Like I told you, the cell service sucks out here."

I eyed the plastic bag as I approached it, and then I ripped it from the post. Sure enough, it was the Glad baggie Beatrice had used for Jacques's treats, only now she'd shoved a note inside. She'd written only two lines on the old Stop-N-Go receipt: *Took Jacques for a ride. Might be awhile.* She'd even dotted her I's with smiley faces.

"I guess Beatrice and the dog are best friends now," I said. "Go figure."

Hollis joined me on the dock and quickly read the note over my shoulder. "Jacques loves to go for boat rides. He probably hopped in the back when she wasn't looking, and then she couldn't get rid of him."

"Sounds about right." While I didn't have to worry about Beatrice, since she'd navigated the Atchafalaya a thousand times over, I faced a new predicament: how to get back to town. I probably had a million e-mails waiting for me at my studio, not to mention an equal number of voice mails on the store's landline.

"Hollis, I'm afraid I have to get back to work. Do you have any idea where I can catch a ride to town?"

He thought it over. "You can always use Granny's old Jeep. We keep it in the storage shed for emergencies. I'm sure she wouldn't mind if y'all borrowed it."

"Thanks, Hollis." I threw him a grateful smile. That was one of the best things about living south of the Mason-Dixon Line. The people were so generous. It didn't matter if someone belonged to your family or not; everyone looked out for each other as a matter of course. "Lead the way."

Hollis turned, and then he headed for a path that led uphill. It was a beautiful day for a hike anyway, so I happily fell in line behind him. Not only did the top of my head feel wonderful with the warm sun on it, but the soft breeze moving through the tupelos kept the mosquitos at bay.

"Say, Hollis. Do you wanna hear a fun fact?" I wanted to keep the conversation going, since he was helping me out of a jam.

"Sure," he called over his shoulder.

"Guess what people used to use for mosquito spray?"

"I have no idea. What?"

"Alligator oil!" I waited for my comment to sink in. "They rubbed alligator oil on their arms and backs, like it was Off or something. They learned that trick from the Indians."

Hollis pretended to shudder. "That's kinda gross, Miss DuBois. To tell you the truth, alligators stink."

"Do tell."

"Yeah. They smell like bad meat." He still spoke over his shoulder as he walked. "It's from all the dead animals in their stomachs."

Now it was my turn to shudder; only my shudder was real. "How could you possibly know such a thing?"

"Easy...I used to swim with the 'gators, back when I was little."

Hollis tossed out that last tidbit as if it was no big deal. As if swimming with alligators was something everyone should try.

"C'mon...you've got to be kidding." I hurried to catch up with him so I could read his face and tell if he was lying or not. "You really used to swim with alligators?"

"Yup. I waited until the weather got chilly. Kinda like now. It's when they start to hibernate. They get so lazy, you can toss food right at 'em and they won't even bite."

It didn't look like he was lying. In fact, Hollis stared straight ahead and never once blinked, which was a sure sign he was telling the truth.

"Well, now. Your fact's even more fun than mine."

We fell into a companionable silence after that, our strides evenly matched. Soon we reached a plot of land that lay behind Ruby's house, where she'd planted a small kitchen garden. The soil held lettuce, carrots, and tomatoes—among other plants—judging by the seed packets she'd glued to the plant stakes.

Hollis paused by a stretch of chicken wire that wound around the garden. "This here is Granny's pride and joy. She's got a real green thumb when it comes to growing plants."

"I can see that." I almost reminded Hollis of the time a killer tried to use his grandmother's garden for a more sinister purpose—and nearly got away with it too—only it was too nice a day to bring up such a dark subject.

Instead, I focused on the lush scenery all around me. A length of scrub brush created a natural hedge to separate the garden from the path, and clumps of emerald sedge provided a soft carpet for my feet. Once we rounded the far corner of the hedge, I spied a surface road that was covered in crushed gravel instead of the clumpy sedge, which we walked toward.

It looked like a county road. Even though Beatrice had insisted on using a pirogue to reach Ruby, it seemed there was a perfectly good surface road right behind the property. The back road probably provided fire trucks, police cars, and emergency vehicles a safe way to reach the residents in times of disaster.

The road split in two a few yards ahead. From what I could tell, a thicket blocked one of the paths, but the other path stood wide open.

Hollis chose the wide-open path, and then he disappeared around the bend.

"Hollis?"

Once I ditched around the bend too, I found myself on another part of the river. Apparently, Ruby's mobile home sat smack-dab in the middle of an isthmus, with water on both sides.

"This is so cool," I said. "It's like you're on an island."

"Pretty much. And the Jeep's over there." He pointed to a toolshed that sat across the river. "It's behind those bushes."

I shielded my eyes from the sun, hoping to spy the shed. Shards of light glanced off the glassy water, which made it hard to see much of anything.

So, I lowered my gaze and tried again. This time, though, something else caught my attention. It was a brown knob, which protruded from the water on a clump of bright green hydrilla.

"What do you think that is?" I pointed to it.

The brown knob provided the only color on the floating plant. It was either a tree stump or the snout of a sleeping alligator, and I sincerely hoped it *wasn't* the latter.

"Could be anything." Hollis's gaze followed mine. "Like I said, the alligators start to hibernate right about now. Lemme see."

He moved south, taking care to lift one of his tennis shoes, and then the other, over an exposed tree root. When he reached the water, he waded in up to his ankles.

"Hollis, come back here! You're going to ruin your shoes!" Which was nothing compared to what *could* happen if the brown spot turned out to be a sleeping alligator, after all.

"I'm okay." He didn't sound concerned, even though the animal slept only a few feet away from him. "I told you, these guys won't hurt me. I grew up swimming around here."

As if to prove his point, he shoved his fingers in his mouth and let out a sharp whistle.

"Hollis! Don't do that! He's not a dog, for gosh sakes."

But hallelujah, the gator didn't stir. Although I could picture the animal's massive jaws snapping out of the water, I kicked off my flats anyway and waded to where Hollis stood.

"I really need to get back to work." I coaxed him back to the shore. "Why don't we leave the alligator alone?"

Hollis didn't budge, though. He stared at the brown knob, entranced. After a moment, he plunged forward, and the top of his head immediately disappeared.

"Hollis! Get back here!"

It was too late, though. He'd been swallowed whole by the glimmering water.

"I mean it, Hollis. Come back!"

Just when I moved to fetch him, his head bobbed up again, but this time his eyes were wild with fright. "Call the police!" he sputtered. "Quick!" He flailed his arms about, as if he wanted to grasp something under the water, only he couldn't quite reach it.

"Wait...what?"

He disappeared again, and when he reemerged, he held something brown and slimy in his left hand. It was a shoe, of all things. An old shoe. A clog, maybe?

"What is that?" I yelled.

"It's Granny's gardening shoe. She's down there, but I can't reach her."

Everything slowed at that moment. Hollis once more plunged under the water, the river erased all signs of him, and my scream tore through the hedges all around us.

Chapter 3

The next few moments passed in a blur. When Hollis realized he couldn't budge his grandmother from her watery grave, he finally gave up and splashed to the surface again.

"Hollis!" I stood still, since my legs refused to work right. It was as if his words had paralyzed me, and all I could do was watch him bob up and down.

Finally, he windmilled his arms to propel himself to shore, and then he stumbled forward and collapsed on the riverbank.

"*Uuuggghhh*," he groaned.

"Hold on, Hollis." I moved back to the shore too, and reached for my cell, which I'd stashed in the pocket of my khakis. It was time to find a cell tower—any cell tower—and try to call for help.

I jabbed at a number for the Louisiana State Police Department, which I kept on speed dial. Unfortunately, my hand shook so much my finger slipped right off the screen. After mumbling a quick prayer for strength, I took a deep breath and tried again, and this time the call went through.

Lance will know what to do. The detective always came to my aid whenever I stumbled across a dead body, which happened a lot more often than one would think, although that was neither here nor there at the moment.

The call crackled and fizzed, but it finally connected me with Lance's phone. He answered on the second ring.

"Hey there, Missy." His voice was warm and welcoming.

"Lance?"

"Okay, what's wrong?" After only one word from me, his tone instantly changed. "Where are you?"

When I didn't answer, he spoke again. "Listen to me. Take a deep breath. I want to hear you breathe."

I did as he asked and gulped some air. "How's that?"

"Better. Now, take it slow. Where are you?"

"There's been an accident, Lance. A terrible accident."

"Are you okay? Tell me what happened."

I turned my back on Hollis, since I didn't want the boy to overhear my conversation. Now that he'd left the water, Hollis had begun to shiver, which meant he was slipping into shock. No need to compound the problem by making him listen to my replay of the last few seconds.

"It's Ruby Oubre," I said. "I came out to her house this morning." After taking so many breaths, I'd almost worked the panic out of my voice. *Almost.*

"She lives by the Atchafalaya River basin, right? Is that where you are now?"

"Yes. I'm here on some land she owns behind the house. I think she drowned, Lance."

"Okay. I'll track your location. Are you anywhere near the surface road?"

"Um-hmm. And I'm with her grandson, Hollis. He's the one who found her body in the first place."

When Hollis groaned again, I regretted not lowering my voice even more. "He's slipping into shock, Lance. Please hurry."

"I'm calling for a car now. You and the boy stay put. We'll be out there as quick as we can."

"Please don't hang up." Like always, I wanted to hear Lance's voice while I waited. It comforted me to know he was on the other end of the phone, no matter how crackly our connection.

"I'm afraid I have to hang up," he said. "But you'll be fine. Just stay put."

"Okay. Whatever you say." Reluctantly, I hung up from the call and turned to face Hollis. "The police will be here soon. Are you going to be okay?"

Hollis didn't answer me. Instead, he stared at the river, as if he fully expected his grandmother to rise out of it. So, I walked over to him, taking care not to make any sudden moves. "It's okay, Hollis. I'm here." I gently placed my hand on his quaking shoulder.

He didn't move...he didn't turn...he didn't acknowledge me.

"Hollis?"

Since he couldn't, or wouldn't, hear me, I was running out of options. *Unless...*

Slowly, I lifted my phone again. *To heck with the crummy cell phone service.* There was one more call I needed to make, one more person who might be able to help me.

I searched for a different number in the phone's speed dial. My fiancé owned the studio next door to mine, where he designed custom ball gowns for high-end weddings. Although it was lunchtime, I knew Ambrose would be in his studio, working on his designs.

Hallelujah, he answered the phone on the second ring.

"Hi, Missy. Don't worry, I didn't forget to eat lunch. I was going—"

"Uh, Ambrose?" This was no time for niceties. "I have to tell you something."

"What's wrong?" Like Lance, his tone immediately changed when he sensed danger. "You're not in trouble, are you?"

"No. I'm fine." I softly patted Hollis's shoulder again, before I turned away. "But something's happened out here. I'm on the Atchafalaya River, by Ruby Oubre's place." Some static sounded over the line, but at least the connection held steady. "I went to visit her and her grandson this morning, remember?"

We'd discussed my plans over breakfast, since Ambrose and I shared what the locals called a "rent house." Although we kept separate bedrooms, that arrangement would end soon enough, once we got married next year.

"Sure. I remember what you told me," he said. "You were going to meet with Hollis about a business venture. So, what happened?"

I struggled to focus. Everything was a blur, which made it hard to stack the details in the right order. "First of all, don't worry about me. I'm fine." I glanced at Hollis to make sure he wasn't listening. "But Ruby is dead. She drowned. I called Lance, and he's coming right over."

A low gasp sounded on the other end. "That's horrible! Stay put, and I'll come too."

Much as I longed to see Ambrose, I knew it wouldn't do any good. "That's okay, honey. There's nothing you can do out here. But Hollis is slipping into shock. Will you talk to him for a few minutes?"

"Of course. Put him on."

I lowered the phone and gently pressed it against Hollis's ear. "It's Ambrose," I whispered. "He wants to tell you something."

The sound of Ambrose's voice traveled over the receiver. Although I couldn't make out the words, Hollis listened intently, and then he nodded at something or other Ambrose had said.

Once their conversation ended, Hollis leaned back from the phone. By now, he'd lost the blank stare and he looked almost resigned to the situation.

I brought the phone back to my ear. "I think you got through to him. What'd you say?"

"I reminded him he needed to stay strong, for his grandmother's sake. He's a good kid. He'll make it through this."

"I hope so." Unlike my fiancé, I wasn't so sure. "I have another favor to ask. Could you please call Beatrice and tell her what's happened?"

"But I thought she'd be with you."

"No. She took the boat to her aunt's house while I worked with Hollis. Now she's out on the river somewhere."

"Okay, I'll try. Maybe I'll check with some of her family. They might have a landline I can call, since this connection is pretty crappy. Do you want Beatrice to meet you somewhere?"

"No. She might as well go back to the hat shop. She can't do anything here either."

"Gotcha. By the way..." He paused, clearly unsure whether he should voice his next thought. "You know you have a terrible knack for finding dead bodies, don't you?"

"Tell me about it! I'm surprised Lance even takes my calls anymore. But this one hurts. I came out here to do Ruby a favor, but I never expected this."

"You poor thing." His voice dripped concern. "Are you sure you don't want me to drive down there and wait with you?"

"No, that's okay." Much as I wanted to see him, there wasn't anything he—or anyone else, for that matter—could do. "Lance will be here any minute, and I'll have to wait while they dredge up the body. Talking to you helps."

"Okay, sweetie. But call me once Lance gets there. I want to make sure you're safe."

"Of course." No doubt, Ambrose also wanted to make sure I didn't overdo things, since I tended to get involved with Lance's police investigations. *Speaking of which...*

"Oh, shine! I just thought of something else."

"What's wrong?" he asked.

"How do we know this wasn't deliberate? Ruby knew how to swim, Ambrose. She told me so herself when I spoke with her the other night. Lance will have to conduct a police investigation."

"Missy..." It was the same tone he always used whenever he wanted to save me from myself. "Let the police handle it this time, okay?"

"Hmmm. We'll see." While I couldn't lie to Ambrose, I *could* be evasive. "There's no telling what Lance will find. Look, I've gotta go. I love you, honey."

With that, I tapped the screen to end the call. Although I'd turned away from Hollis, I could tell he'd eavesdropped on the conversation, since he tilted his head toward me.

"By any chance, did you hear what I said?" I asked.

"Maybe." He sounded miserable. "Okay, I did. And you're right... Granny knew how to swim. So, how'd she end up at the bottom of the river? It doesn't make sense."

"I don't know. But let's not jump to conclusions, okay? The police will be here any minute, and they'll know what to do."

Fortunately, the sound of police sirens reached us only a few moments later. The noise grew louder and louder, the cacophony accompanied by staccato red lights that slashed through the tupelos overhead.

"Praise the Lord," I said. "They're here."

The noise gave way to the crunch of rubber tires on pea gravel as cars skidded to a stop on the surface road.

"We're over here!" I yelled, as soon as someone's door screeched open and closed. "Down by the river."

Lance appeared first. He quickly rounded the bend, his navy-blue police uniform a dark splotch against the tangled kudzu. He must've had an important meeting back at headquarters, because he usually wore blue jeans or khakis whenever he went out to investigate a crime. A tall, handsome African American, he wore his police dress blues well.

He first inspected the placid water, and when he finished, he glanced my way. "There you are."

Several officers followed him through the kudzu, including one who wore a rubber wet suit. A scuba face mask dangled from the diver's neck, and he carried a long stick in his arms.

I didn't move, and I didn't point out where Ruby's body lay. I knew better than that. During every other police investigation, Lance separated me from everyone else before he asked me any questions. That way, my memories wouldn't crisscross with another witness's...like Hollis.

Sure enough, the diver headed for Hollis, while Lance moved to where I stood.

"I'm so glad you're okay," he said, once he reached me.

"I'm fine." I nodded at the teenager. "But you might want to check on him. I think he's going into shock."

"I'll do that in a minute. First things first. Where did you find the body?"

"I didn't find the body. Hollis did. And he found her over there." I pointed to the clump of hydrilla, which bobbed so innocently on the water's surface.

"Did she come to the surface?" Lance asked.

"No, she didn't. Hollis had to struggle to reach her. But he could only touch her shoe, so he gave up."

"Gotcha." Lance cast another knowing look at the water. After pulling a pen from the pocket of his uniform, he followed it up with a slim notebook. "You know I'll need to take you to the police station to videotape your statement. And it'll take us awhile to secure the area." He scribbled a few notes as he spoke.

"Of course. But, Lance...what do you think happened?"

He didn't answer. Instead, once he finished writing, he scanned the river again. This time, his gaze lingered on the floating hydrilla.

Not that I wanted to be nosy—*okay, maybe a little nosy*—but he seemed to be going through a checklist in his mind. And, knowing Lance, he'd already connected enough of the dots to put together a rough picture of the crime.

"I know you, Lance. You think something's wrong, don't you?"

"Let's not jump the gun."

"But this doesn't make sense. Ruby knew how to swim."

Lance threw me a look. "*You're* jumping the gun. The ME will do an autopsy today, maybe tomorrow. We'll get the summary report first, like we always do. In the meantime, why don't you head over to my police cruiser and wait for me there."

He jerked his thumb back to indicate a shiny new police car. Thank goodness, he didn't expect me to ride back to the station in his Oldsmobile, which he tended to treat like an oversized trash dumpster. Although there were far more important things to worry about, I didn't relish the thought of sitting next to a week's worth of Cheetos wrappers and Diet Coke cans.

"All right. I'll head over there and let you do your job in peace."

"Thank you. And there's one more thing. I don't want the boy to be here when we dredge up Ruby's body. He doesn't need to see that."

"But what if he won't leave her?" I'd seen the frantic look on Hollis's face when he realized he couldn't pull his grandmother free.

"He'll *have* to leave her. Like I said, it's something no one should have to see. Drowning victims tend to bloat up once the bacteria invades their organs. The same thing happens to their eyes. They bulge—"

"Okay, okay. I get it." No need for me to picture Ruby's body decomposing in the water only a few steps away. "I'll try my best."

"Thank you. Now might be a good time to distract him, so we can get to work."

As I turned away from Lance, my gaze traveled to the diver and his long pole. He'd already donned the face mask, and he'd telescoped the pole—which stretched about four feet—to twice that length. A sinister-looking hook capped the end of it.

Lance noticed my stare. "We call it a snag bar. The diver will dredge it through the water until it catches on her clothes."

"That's horrible." Especially ominous was a large three-pronged hook at the end, which looked like one of the treble hooks my grandpa used whenever he went fishing.

Lance shrugged. "It's the best system we have for pulling bodies out of shallow water. Otherwise, we'd use a drag bar on the back of a motorboat. But that's only when someone dies in a deep lake, or out in the ocean."

Although Lance sounded perfectly comfortable discussing the various ways police could recover a drowning victim, I'd heard enough. It didn't seem natural to stand on dry land and talk about someone else when their body was slowly disintegrating under the water.

"Hey, Hollis." I quickly moved to the teenager. "I forgot something back at your house. Could you take me back there, please?"

The boy didn't respond. He still looked shell-shocked, as if he had no idea where he was or how long he'd been there. Although someone had draped a blanket around him, his skinny shoulder blades still trembled.

"Please," I repeated. "I don't remember how to get back to your house."

Finally, his stare snapped. "But I can't leave her down there. Grandma needs me."

"Oh, honey." My heart hurt for him. "She doesn't need you anymore. There's nothing you can do. And we've got to let the police do their jobs. Please."

Cautiously, I took Hollis by the hand and slowly turned him away from the scene. Neither of us spoke as we began to shuffle slowly back to the mobile home. What was there to say?

The day had started off so well. Hollis couldn't wait to tell me all about his new business, which he hoped would attract tourists from far and wide. After all, how many chances did people have to observe a real-live alligator in its natural habitat?

But when one of the "alligators" turned out to be something far more sinister, the day had taken an ominous turn. And neither of us knew how to right it again.

Chapter 4

I numbly trudged ahead of Hollis on the surface road, sneaking a peek back every so often to make sure he was okay.

Once again, the marshland was eerily quiet, with only the *whoosh* of a soft breeze and the *crunch* of our footsteps on the gravel road.

When we finally arrived at the mobile home, I discovered one of the reasons it seemed so quiet. Beatrice hadn't returned yet, and nothing disturbed the water but a few dragonflies that dipped and swooped over its surface.

Where could she be?

Lost in thought, I climbed the rickety steps and entered the house. The front room seemed even darker now, since afternoon shadows painted the furniture gray. Even the newspapers, which splattered across the couch and floor, looked like muddied throw rugs someone had tossed there by accident. The newspapers gave me an idea, though.

"There it is." I grabbed indiscriminately for a section of newsprint and glanced at the headline. "This is why I had to come back. To get the…um… sports section. Yeah, that's it. I'd promised Ambrose I'd bring him the sports section from today's paper, since ours didn't get delivered. Do you mind?"

"What?" Hollis once more looked confused, as if he didn't quite understand the question. "You want to borrow the newspaper? Okay…I guess so."

"Thank you. And do you mind if I use your bathroom too?"

This time, I didn't wait for a response. Instead, I trundled down the hall and slid into the restroom, where I pretended to be busy for a good five minutes, since I needed time for the police diver to finish his grisly task.

I dillydallied for an extra minute or two in front of the mirror, knowing full well Hollis would never question me when I returned. He'd be too embarrassed, and he no doubt had a million other things on his mind at the moment.

When I finally emerged from the bathroom, I shoved the newspaper in my back pocket. "All set. Guess it's time to go back to Lance." I also glanced at my watch, which put the time at one o'clock. "He wants to take us to the police station, so he can videotape our statements."

"Sure. I guess so. Whatever."

Hollis moved on autopilot to the screen door. Instead of swinging it open, though, he paused on the threshold.

"Do you think I should lock the place up?" His gaze flitted around the room. "There's not a whole lot to steal, but that's what Grandma used to do."

I nodded gently. "Yes, you probably should. We might be gone an hour or so. I think you should call your relatives too, once we get to the police station. You need to let them know what happened."

"My what? Oh yeah. Relatives." While he parroted the words back to me, I could tell he wasn't listening.

"Yes, you should call your relatives," I repeated. "Maybe there's an aunt, or an uncle?"

"Well, Grandma was pretty old. She didn't have a lot of relatives left. I think she had a sister up in Baton Rouge, though."

"Good. Why don't you think about the best way to reach her, while I lock all the doors." I lifted what I guessed to be a house key from its place on a cup hook nailed to the wall. "This will only take me a second."

I hung back a bit as I surveyed the room one last time. Since I really didn't know when we'd return—I'd only guessed at how much time Lance would need at the police station—maybe I should straighten things up a bit.

It was the only way I could think of to honor her memory. Even though Ruby didn't seem like the type who cared what other people thought about her, I did. Before long, countless people would trudge through the front door, including crime scene investigators, neighbors, and long-lost relatives, and I didn't want them to think Ruby was a slob. While I didn't plan to disturb the scene too much, since Lance would no doubt include the home in his police investigation, it wouldn't hurt to shuffle the newspapers into a neat pile.

The front section was lying on the ground, so I bent to retrieve it. As I straightened, though, I nearly cracked my head on the corner of a glass coffee table that was half-hidden by the debris.

Sweet mother of pearl! The last things I needed were a goose egg on my forehead and a splitting headache.

I pushed the table back a bit, and that's when I noticed an official-looking document on its surface. A colorful logo for Dupre Realty, Inc., scrolled across the page.

Now, I'd known Hank Dupre for several years, mainly because he bought an old mansion near my rent house and he's also Beatrice's uncle. Not a week went by that Hank didn't drop by the hat studio to say hey to Beatrice or maybe grab a cup of coffee.

Now, why would Hank correspond with Ruby? And why would she leave his letter lying around so willy-nilly? Curious, I bent over the paper, which had nice, large type that allowed me to read every word.

The purpose of this letter of intent is to set forth conditions
and terms for the purchase of your property...

"Purchase?" I quickly glanced up, but Hollis had disappeared. He'd already stepped through the screen door, judging by the way the mesh vibrated in his wake.

Granted, now was not the best time, nor the best place, for me to satiate my curious nature, but questions kept flitting through my mind.

Why would someone want to buy Ruby's place?

Heaven only knew it wasn't for the curb appeal since mold limned the mobile home and its foundation rested on cinder blocks. But that didn't mean someone wouldn't find the land underneath it irresistible.

But why didn't anyone in town mention this?

I hadn't heard a word from friends, customers, or fellow shopkeepers, all of which meant I should track down Hank when I returned to Crowning Glory, since it might quiet the funny feeling that tickled my stomach.

I headed for the front door, which I locked behind me, and then I rejoined Hollis, who waited at the foot of the stairs. I even whipped out the sports section from my back pocket to show him our visit wasn't a total ruse.

"All set. Ambrose will read every word of this section. Let's go catch up with Lance."

Hollis didn't move, though. He looked even more troubled than before, his eyes drawn to the ground around his feet.

"Are you okay, Hollis?"

"It's just..." His voice trailed off miserably.

"What's wrong? You know you can tell me anything."

"It's just that I'm...I'm scared. I've never been to a police station before. What if I mess up?"

The poor boy. I reached out to touch his shoulder. "It's okay. I'll be at the station too, so you won't be alone."

"I know. But what about afterward?"

"Why, afterward I'll come back here with you. I won't leave you alone today."

"Promise?"

"Cross my heart. We'll figure this out."

I shoved the newspaper back in my pocket, and then I motioned for him to follow me. As we trudged along the surface road, we passed the kitchen garden and then we reached the tip of the wooded isthmus.

After a while, we arrived at the point where the surface road split in two.

It was the same two trails we'd seen before. But this time, a trio of police cruisers blocked the entrance to the path on the right, and an ominous white van painted with the blocky logo for the St. James Parish Coroner's Office sat nearby. The van's doors stood wide open, and the shiny tip of a metal gurney glinted in the darkness.

Uh-oh. Hollis doesn't need to see that.

"Look over there. It's Lance's police cruiser." I pointed to the first car in the lineup, since I wanted to distract Hollis from the van's open doors. "Do you want to ride shotgun, and I'll sit in the back?"

He shook his head. "No, I'd rather sit with you."

"Fair enough. Follow me."

We headed for Lance's squad car, where I yanked open the back door and slid onto the vinyl cushion. Hollis followed suit and scooted next to me.

After another few minutes, Lance took his place behind the steering wheel. Once he drove us away from the river, it was only a matter of time before we arrived at the police substation.

Once again, Lance separated Hollis and me as soon as we walked through the plate-glass door, which bothered Hollis to no end, until he realized Lance was only following police procedure. Then, Lance videotaped our statements one at a time.

Although the interview room was anything but cozy, with white walls, regulation armchairs, and a chipped laminate conference table, my eyes began to droop as the interview dragged on. While adrenaline had coursed through my body all morning, the hormone was nowhere to be found by the time the camera's red light blinked off, and I desperately wanted a nap.

In fact, I could barely keep my eyes open, even during the ride back to Ruby's house. All I wanted was a hot shower and a cool pillow and to forget the events of the past few hours.

Hollis must've felt the same way, because he nodded off on my shoulder during the ride. I gently nudged him awake when Lance pulled the cruiser behind Ruby's mobile home.

"Where…where are we?" He groggily straightened as the car rolled to a stop.

"We're back at your granny's place," I said.

"Huh?"

It was the same confused expression I'd seen all day, including that moment when he woke up to find Beatrice and me standing in his front yard.

"Lance brought you back home." I spoke as gently as I could. "He gave us a ride from the police station, after he took our statements."

That woke him up, and he roughly rubbed the sleep from his eyes. "You know, you don't have to go back inside with me, Miss DuBois. You already told me you needed to get back to work."

"Are you kidding?" I softly *tsk*ed. "There's no way I'd let you come back here by yourself. Let's get you settled in, and then I'll think about other things."

"No, really," he said. "It's okay. Granny used to leave me alone all the time. I don't mind."

"Yeah, but this is different." I glanced toward the front seat, where I met Lance's gaze in the rearview mirror. Apparently, he'd been listening to our conversation. "Thanks for the ride, Lance. Could you please let Ambrose know where I am so he doesn't worry about me? I forgot to call him when we were at the police station. I've been a hot mess ever since… well, you know."

"No problem." His gaze shifted to Hollis. "You sure you're going to be okay, son? You can always wait for your relatives back at the station."

"No, I'm okay. I'd rather be here." Hollis swung open the car door and slowly stepped onto the gravel road.

I did the same, and then we both watched Lance pull away from the house. Soon, the only thing visible on the cruiser were its red taillights, which whittled down to pinpoints of light after a moment or two.

"Hey, I've got an idea." It was time to say something, anything, to distract the boy. "Neither of us has had a bite to eat today. I don't know about you, but I'm starving. Want me to make us something?"

He gave a half-hearted nod. "Sure, I guess. Why not?"

We turned toward the house, and then we slowly made our way around the kitchen garden. Just as we were about to broach a corner of the building, something loud crashed on the other side of it.

Hollis jerked his head around. "What was that?"

"Maybe Beatrice is back," I said, hopefully. "Wouldn't that be something?"

While I didn't expect to see her—I'd even told Ambrose to send her back to the studio—part of me hoped it was true. Beatrice could help me out here. She could tell the neighbors about Ruby's death, since she knew everyone up and down the river, and she could help me console the boy.

My heart quickened at the thought. *That's it. Together, Beatrice and I will tell people what happened, and then we'll try to make Hollis feel better.* "C'mon, Hollis. Let's go find her."

I hurried around the corner, fully expecting to see Beatrice waiting for me in the pirogue, with an exuberant dog slobbering on the seat next to her.

But my heart sank when I finally reached the dock. An old man—not Beatrice—leaned over the weathered planks, one leg thrust forward as he reached for something he'd dropped there. He wore boat shoes, judging by the thick rubber soles, and a bright orange camp shirt, which played up a sunburn on his arms and neck.

Apparently, he was trying to reach a flashlight, which lolled on the edge of the dock. Thick and shiny, the cylinder looked like a contractor's flashlight, with a heavy handle and a lens as big as a salad plate. The flashlight rolled tantalizingly close to the edge of the dock before it stopped.

"Excuse me," I called as I moved forward. "Can I help you?"

The stranger didn't turn. Instead, he grabbed the flashlight and plucked it up in the nick of time.

He probably didn't hear me.

I glanced back at Hollis. "Were you expecting someone?"

"Son of a bitch—"

"Hollis!" He'd never sworn around me before and, quite frankly, I didn't like it. "What's wrong with you?"

"He's…he's not supposed to be here."

"What do you mean? Who's 'he'?"

Hollis didn't answer. Instead, he glared at the stranger's back as if he wanted to push the man right into the river.

"Who is it?" I repeated.

Still no answer. Since Hollis couldn't—or wouldn't—answer me, I had no choice. Today was *not* the day for someone to traipse onto Ruby's property all willy-nilly and upset her one and only grandson.

So, I sprinted across the dock, prepared to run interference between Hollis and this unwelcome guest.

"Pardon me." I quickly tapped the man's shoulder when I reached him. "Can I help you?"

That did the trick. The stranger whirled around, as if he'd been confronted with a ghost. "What'n the blazes...?"

"Whoa." I automatically reared back. The man loomed over me—he stood at least six-foot-five—and he brandished the flashlight like a weapon.

"Gah-lee," he said. "Don'tcha know ya can't go sneakin' up on folks like that?"

"I'm so sorry. I didn't mean to scare you."

"What're you doing here?" Hollis's voice boomed behind me.

"Hey there, Hollis." The man finally lowered the flashlight. "Didn't see ya standing there. Let me turn ma ears up." With that, he reached for something behind his left ear and fiddled with it until he was satisfied. "There. That's better. Had to turn up the ol' hearing aids. Now, who's yer friend?"

"None of your business," Hollis said.

I threw Hollis a look as I extended my hand. *No need to be rude.* "Hello...I'm Melissa DuBois. But everyone calls me Missy."

"Nice to meet ya. I'm Cap'n Gaudet," The visitor placed a weathered palm in mine, his skin rough and raw. "I run swamp boat tours around here."

"Nice to meet you too." I glanced at a pocket on the man's shirt, where a grinning alligator lounged beneath the words BLEW-BY-YOU BOAT TOURS. The alligator wore a jaunty sailor's cap and a wide smile.

"Yep," the boat captain said, "ah've been running tours around this here swamp before either of you was born." His eyes disappeared into a patchwork of wrinkles when he chuckled.

Hollis didn't seem amused, though. "Whatcha doing here, Cap'n? You must've heard about what happened this morning."

"I did. I did, indeed." The captain's smile faltered. "It's a terrible shame, son. A downright, terrible shame."

"Really?" Hollis said. "I would've thought you'd be dancing in the streets right about now."

"Hollis!" I shot him another look. Although he had every right to be upset about his grandmother's death, he didn't have the right to take it out on the people around him. Especially since the boat captain seemed harmless enough. "That's not a very nice thing to say."

"Not very nice?" he answered. "You don't know who this is, Miss DuBois."

Again, I'd never heard Hollis use that tone before. "Yes, I do. He said he runs swamp tours around here. Seems to me he just wanted to pay you a visit."

"A visit?" Hollis scoffed. "*Ppppfffttt.* Is that why you're here, Cap'n? Did you bring me a casserole? You came to comfort me in my time of need?"

"Now, son," the man answered. "There's no reason for you to get all hot under the collar. I had sum business downstream, so I thought I'd come by and pay my respects. Dat's all there is to it. Nothin' more."

"Captain, with you there's always more." Hollis cut his gaze to the industrial-strength flashlight. "Do you usually bring your toolbox along when you come out for a visit? Looks to me like you were checking under Granny's dock. I betcha have a tape measure in your other pocket, don't you?"

The captain didn't respond, but he didn't deny it, either.

"You've always wanted this land, haven't you?" Hollis continued. "My guess is you're here to measure the property and check out the pilings. Tell her, Cap'n."

Finally, Captain Gaudet dropped the phony smile. "Maybe there's a little bit of truth to that. A tiny bit. But I mostly wanted to see how yer gettin' on."

"Don't lie," Hollis said. "You only have one thing on your mind. It's no secret you want to dock one of your boats out here."

"That's enough, Hollis." I said. Whether or not it was true, this argument wasn't doing anyone a lick of good. "Let's go back to the house. I promised I'd make you that meal, remember?"

I reached for Hollis's arm, but he stepped away.

"Why, I oughta…"

"You oughta what, son?" Slowly, the captain raised the heavy flashlight again. "You gonna take me on?"

"I might just do that," Hollis replied.

Although the teenager was a good fifty years younger than his opponent, there was no telling what could happen, and I wasn't in the mood to find out.

"Okay, gentlemen. That's enough. Let's take this down a notch. We're all friends here."

When neither of them moved, I spoke again. "I mean it. It's time to go back to your neutral corners. We'll start with you, Captain. Why don't you take whatever boat you used to get here, and leave. There's nothing for you to see."

The flashlight wobbled a bit in the captain's hands, but he didn't lower it.

"Hollis, please." I turned to the teenager, since I was running out of options. "Come into the house with me. We need to get something to eat. Let it go for now."

After what felt like an eternity, Hollis finally exhaled. "Okay, fine, but this guy better keep away from Granny's property. I see him come back, and I'm gonna call the police."

"Will ya, now?" the old man jeered. "You jus' do that, son. I doubt they'll come runnin' for sum punk like you."

"I said that's enough." I took Hollis by the arm and pulled him away from the boat captain. Although he glanced back a time or two, Hollis didn't try to escape my grasp.

By the time we reached the house, something loud roared to life behind us. Given the deafening noise, it sounded like an airboat. The captain must've ridden an airboat to Ruby's property and docked it downstream, even though he had a perfectly good dock available nearby.

I snuck a quick glance behind me. Sure enough, a black airboat churned through the water, about five hundred yards away. On its end sat a giant propeller that whirled around like an oversized fan blade.

"No wonder he's so hard of hearing!" I yelled to Hollis.

The teen nodded. "He's been like that forever. Deaf as anything without his hearing aid."

We watched the spectacle churn through the water, until the boat disappeared behind a stand of tupelos.

"Why didn't he just use your dock?" I lowered my voice, although the noise still rumbled around us.

"Why do you think? He didn't want anyone to know he was here."

"That settles it. There's no way I'm going to let you stay here by yourself tonight. You're coming back to my rent house. You can stay in Ambrose's room. And I won't take no for an answer...so don't even try it."

Hollis started to protest, but then he relented. Either he knew it was no use to argue with me, or he was spooked by the confrontation on the dock. "You sure you won't mind?"

"Not at all. I insist. Go grab your things, and I'll meet you here when you're done."

I scrambled up the steps and unlocked the door, since I still had the house key in my pocket, and then I retreated down the stairs again.

"Now, get your stuff." I spoke quickly, before either of us could change our minds. "Ambrose won't mind. I bring home surprises all the time."

Although I hadn't asked my fiancé, I wasn't worried about Ambrose. He trusted me. Besides...what could possibly go wrong if we opened our home to a teenager in need?

Chapter 5

Once Hollis left to get his things inside the mobile home, I fished my cell from the pocket of my khakis again.

To be honest, I'd had enough drama for one day, and I longed to hear a friendly voice. Even if that meant putting up with iffy cell phone service or static on the line.

I punched a number on my speed dial, and sure enough, the call finally connected, after a false start or two. The line hissed and crackled, but at least it connected me with Ambrose's cell phone after a bit.

He answered on the second ring. "Hey, darlin'. Whatcha doing?"

I could picture him sitting at his drafting table at work, his broad hands hovering over some complicated design for a custom ball gown. Somehow, those masculine hands could conjure a work of art from everyday sewing materials like lace, sequins, and silk jacquard. It was one of the many reasons I loved him so much.

"Mostly, I'm missing you, and I'm still at Ruby's place."

No need for me to explain what'd happened. By now, half of Bleu Bayou knew all about Ruby's drowning and the way police retrieved her body, and the other half would find out about it by nightfall. That was the thing about living in a small town. News traveled at the speed of light. Or, as we liked to say, it traveled at the speed of boredom.

"Stay right there. I'm coming to get you. It'll take me about ten minutes if I leave right now."

"Do you mind? I told Hollis I'd make him something to eat, but this place is starting to give me the creeps. I'm sure you're probably working—"

"Missy." His tone silenced my protests. "Not another word. I'll lock up the studio and head over to Ruby's."

With that, he clicked off the line, prepared to drop everything else to help me out.

I'm the luckiest girl in the world—

"Are you okay?" Hollis stood in the doorway of the mobile home, and his voice brought me back to reality.

"Yeah, I'm fine." I shook my head to clear it. "Why do you ask?"

"Because you just sighed. Are you sure everything's okay?"

"I'm sure. Ambrose's coming to pick us up. He'll be here in about ten minutes."

That gave me plenty of time to put the property to rights again. Once I helped Hollis drag his duffel bag out of the house, I locked the front door, and then I headed for the statue of the Blessed Virgin, where I said a prayer for Ruby. By the time Ambrose's car pulled onto the property, twilight had settled over the clouds, and it silvered the black paint on the Audi's hood.

I hurried over to the driver's side as soon as he parked, and then I waited for him to lower the window.

"It's so good to see you!" I leaned over and gave him a quick kiss.

"You too, sweetheart. By the way, the news is all over town about Ruby."

"I'm sure it is. We already had someone come out here today. It was a riverboat captain who wanted to check out the property. Hollis was livid. I'll tell you the story on the way back."

After another quick kiss, I moved around the hood of the car and signaled for Hollis to jump into the back seat. He tossed his duffel in first, then he dove in after it, while I settled in next to Ambrose.

I waited until we reached the end of the surface road before I leaned toward him.

"You sure you're okay with all this?" I whispered. "It'll only be for a few days. Promise. Just until we figure out what's going on with Ruby and the police investigation."

"Of course." Ambrose cut his gaze to the rearview mirror, just like Lance had done. "I'm happy to have you stay with us, Hollis. Take as long as you want."

I sighed again. "I knew you'd say that." Even though Ambrose didn't know why I'd first invited Hollis to come stay with us, he never questioned me. "You wouldn't believe what happened after we came back from the police station today."

With that, I proceeded to tell him all about the scene with Captain Gaudet. By the time I reached the point where the old man threatened Hollis with a flashlight, the shadowy outline of Bleu Bayou's business district appeared up ahead.

"Hmmm." I stopped my story midsentence. The building that housed my studio, Crowning Glory, rose regally above the rest. A former spice factory, developers had converted it into a series of upscale bridal shops: everything from a photo studio and bakery to a justice of the peace and my millinery shop. We nicknamed the building "the Factory," and brides came from near and far to visit it.

After all, who wouldn't want to get married on the Great River Road? Several restored antebellum mansions lined the banks of the Mississippi River here. Brides had their choice of emerald-green lawns that stretched for days, grand Doric columns that soared to the sky, and wraparound porches that took full advantage of the views. If ever a place fulfilled someone's wish for a fairy-tale wedding, it was one of the mansions on the Great River Road.

"You know…" My voice trailed off as we approached the Factory.

"Is something wrong?" Ambrose asked.

"No, not really. It's just that I haven't been inside my studio all day. I kinda miss it."

"I get that. It's hard to be gone all day. There's no telling what could happen in the meantime."

The closer we drew to the building, the stronger its pull became. Ambrose was right. Anything could've happened at Crowning Glory while I was on the bayou. Maybe a client waltzed in unannounced. Or a supplier ran out of material for an order. And what if someone cancelled an order at the last minute, which would leave me stuck with a custom creation and no one to give it to?

Although Beatrice had returned to the studio at some point, my assistant didn't like to bother me with petty problems. Which I appreciated, until a "petty" problem blossomed into a full-scale disaster, which'd been known to happen.

"Do you think Hollis would mind if I dashed into Crowning Glory first? Just for a minute or two?"

"Not at all," Ambrose said. "I can take him back to the house while you check in at your shop. Your car's still there, right?"

"Yes. And I won't be long. I just hate to leave Hollis right now."

"You know I can hear you." Hollis leaned over the front seat, a shy smile on his lips. "And I don't mind. You've been so nice to me, Miss DuBois. Please don't change your plans on my account."

"Okay. As long as you're sure you don't mind."

The Factory filled our windshield now, its rough red bricks softened by the setting sun.

"Sounds like we have a plan," Ambrose said. "I'll drop you off at the studio, and then I'll take Hollis back to the house. Don't hurry home on our account. We'll be fine."

I threw him a grateful smile. "To tell you the truth, I don't think I could sleep a wink tonight if I didn't find out what happened at the shop today."

Ambrose pulled the car into the parking lot, and then he drove next to the French door that fronted my studio. The mahogany door shone in the twilight, the finish smooth as satin. I'd replaced the original door back in January, after a crazy person hacked the old one to smithereens. But that was another story for yet another day.

I hopped from the car after Ambrose put it in Park, and then I leaned through the driver's-side window to kiss him again.

"Thanks, honey. I won't be too long. Just long enough to make sure everything's okay." I glanced back at Hollis. "Make yourself at home when you get to our place. We want you to feel comfortable there, okay?"

But Hollis wouldn't look at me. Instead, he studied the bare parking lot through the car's window, as if the gritty pavement suddenly fascinated him.

"Hollis, is something wrong?" I asked.

"Well…" He still wouldn't look at me. "It's just that I never got anything to eat today. I'm kinda hungry."

Oh, shine! "That's right. You didn't get any food, did you?"

"Don't worry about it." Ambrose had been watching our exchange in the rearview mirror. "There's plenty of food at the house. I made a big potful of jambalaya last night, and Bettina brought me a dozen sweet rolls today."

I squelched a smile. "Now there's a surprise."

Bettina LeBlanc, our resident baker at the Factory, always did have a soft spot for Ambrose. She couldn't wait to bring him fresh-baked beignets, warm madeleines, and sugary pecan pies. I liked to tease him about it, only because Bettina had a long-standing membership in AARP, a half-dozen grandchildren, and a headful of dark hair that finally grayed.

I turned away from the car, and then I walked to the front door of my studio. Light poured through the cut-glass panes, which meant one of two things: Either Beatrice was still hard at work inside, or she'd forgotten to turn off the lights again. I sincerely hoped it was the former, because I wanted to hear all about the day's events.

One turn of the doorknob, and I knew the answer. Beatrice stood across the room from me, behind a counter that held our cash register. She faced another woman, only this woman wore a burgundy cashmere sweater over her shoulders and matching riding boots. The visitor perched regally on one of our bar stools, her expensive leather boots about a foot above the floor.

"Hello?" I cautiously entered, since I didn't expect to see a visitor at this late hour.

"You're back." Beatrice breathed the words, obviously relieved. "I didn't think you'd come back today, but I'm so glad you did."

The girl in front of her quickly swiveled around. "So, this must be the owner. It's about time." A stout girl with a broad forehead and wide-set brown eyes, she arched one eyebrow. "Do you always run this late?"

"I'm sorry. Did we have an appointment?" I hurried across the room, since I had no idea what she was talking about.

"I called your studio at lunchtime to make an appointment," she said. "Now that I'm here, I must say your place looks a little more...um...*cozy* than I expected from your website."

"Uh, thank you?" I extended my hand. "I'm Melissa DuBois. Feel free to call me Missy, though, since everyone else does. I'm sorry if you thought I'd be here for your appointment."

"That *is* the normal protocol, isn't it?" The girl sniffed as she returned my handshake. "I'm Sabine d'Aulnay. You've no doubt heard of my family."

The name gave me pause. About a year ago, one of my clients staged an elaborate wedding on a restored riverboat. And not just any riverboat...a famous paddle-wheeler called the *Riverboat Queen*. Its ruby red paint and forest-green accents made it instantly recognizable to anyone who traveled down the Mississippi. And the captain, Christophe d'Aulnay, ran herd over a large and extended family that many considered royalty around these parts.

"Interesting," I responded. "One of my clients rented your father's boat for her wedding."

"Technically, it's a ship." Sabine sniffed again.

"I guess I should've called you," Beatrice said. "But I knew you'd be busy, so I thought I'd handle the appointment by myself."

"That's okay. We didn't have great cell service down at Ruby's place anyway. You might not have been able to reach—"

"This is all very well and good," Sabine interrupted, "but can we please get back to my bridal appointment?"

I noticed she didn't even bother to comment on Ruby's passing, although she had to know about it. Everyone did. "Of course. I take it you're getting married soon?"

"Why else would I be here? By the way...you come highly recommended. You must have a ton of family and friends."

Uh-oh. That was the second backhanded compliment she'd paid me in only a few minutes. First, she referred to my studio as "cozy," which no doubt meant "small," and then she insinuated that only a friend or family member would give me a good review.

Now, I was no stranger to the backhanded compliment, since it was practically an art form here in the South. While a true compliment meant a genuine expression of praise, a backhanded one involved a thinly veiled insult softened by a sugary tone. Some of my favorites included "isn't that special," "I'll pray for you," and the ever-popular "bless your heart."

To be honest, I only used a backhanded compliment when someone deserved it. Too bad Sabine d'Aulnay didn't feel the same way.

"I'm so glad people referred you to me." The best response was to take the high road. "I can give you dozens of references, if you'd like."

"Well, isn't that special. I wouldn't need more than three or four."

"Okay, then. So, you're getting married." I slid onto the bar stool next to hers, prepared to bite my tongue for as long as necessary. "Tell me what you're looking for. Do you have anything special in mind?"

"As a matter of fact…" She reached into an enormous Louis Vuitton she'd placed on her lap. "I know exactly what I want." Out came a dozen glossy magazine pages, which she spooled onto the counter like a colorful quilt.

"Wow. You have quite a collection there."

"I've been thinking about it for a long time." She reached for a certain photo, a half-page ad from Tiffany that showed a diamond tiara inlaid with scores of pale blue stones.

"That's beautiful. There must ten carats' worth of diamonds in there."

"Twelve carats, to be exact. It's something I'm having my jeweler copy. I need you to come up with the rest of the veil, though. Do you think you can do that?"

"Of course." It'd be quite simple, actually. A bit of Chantilly lace, a trim of seed pearls, and *voilà!* The diamonds would pop like starbursts.

"By the way," Sabine said. "Tell me something. Have you ever worked on a veil of this…uh…*quality* before?"

By quality, she no doubt meant "expense," so I nodded. "As a matter of fact, I have. I've done some very high-profile weddings over the years, and some very custom pieces."

"It's true." Beatrice jumped in to defend me, like I knew she would. "She made a veil for the governor's daughter, and she made a gorgeous fascinator for a local newscaster. A lady by the name of Stormie Lanai."

"A newscaster?" Sabine crinkled her nose. "You don't mean that girl who works at KATC, do you? I'm sure she had a nice little affair, but hardly the type of wedding I'm talking about."

Nice little affair? I almost laughed, but I stopped short when I realized she wasn't kidding. Stormie Lanai, who possessed one of the largest egos I'd ever encountered, would never call her wedding a "nice little affair." She was the one who'd asked for a replica of Princess Diana's veil, for heaven's sake. Come to think of it, it'd be fun to put someone like Stormie Lanai in the same room as Sabine d'Aulnay and watch the fireworks go off.

"Well, I've worked for a few more clients you might recognize. I also designed a veil for the Solomon family out of Baton Rouge."

"*Hmpf.* And look how that turned out," Sabine said.

To be fair, that wedding *did* end up with a murder trial, after someone killed the poor bride the night before her nuptials. But that had nothing to do with the beautiful, cathedral-length veil I created for the occasion. It wasn't my fault the Solomon family had more enemies than you could shake a stick at.

"What I meant to say was I've worked for several high-profile clients over the years. Only I prefer not to talk about them, since they appreciate their privacy. You understand, I'm sure."

"Of course. Completely." She'd softened her tone, now that I'd appealed to her vanity. "It's not easy to be well-known around here. Trust me. It may look like fun and games on the outside, but on the inside, it's a lot of work. People expect certain things from you."

"Um-hm."

"And just to be clear," she said. "With this type of budget, you need to provide a certain level of service. If you haven't noticed...money's no object. I'd want you to be on call twenty-four-seven."

No doubt. While part of me wanted to end this appointment right then and there, and escort Sabine from my studio, another part—the practical part—couldn't do it. After all, I had bills to pay, an employee to compensate, and supplies to pay for, like a new door.

Just because I owned a business, it didn't give me carte blanche to do anything I wanted. In fact, quite often the opposite. Sometimes I had to do things I'd rather not do, all in the service of the greater good. I'd tried to explain that to Hollis during our business lesson this morning, although it was anyone's guess whether he understood the concept.

"Of course," I said. "I always try to provide the best service to all my clients."

Apparently satisfied with my answer, Sabine began to shuffle through the puddle of magazine clips again. Once she found what she was looking for, she thrust it under my nose.

It was an ad for the Louisiana Art & Science Museum, which touted a new exhibit based on the movie *Gone with the Wind.*

"This is what I have in mind for my bridesmaids," she said. "There will be twenty of them. Whaddya think?"

The glossy ad showed costumes and props from the movie, including a hat Scarlett O'Hara wore at the start of it. The straw hat featured an enormous brim that extended at least twenty-two inches around. A thick velvet ribbon cinched the material together under the chin.

"It's pretty," I offered. "But have you thought about your wedding photos?"

"My wedding photos? Why would I worry about those?"

"Because when you have a hat brim that big, you need to put space between your bridesmaids. It also means a wide-angled camera lens. Even then, the photographer might not be able to fit everyone into one shot."

"Look." Sabine brusquely snatched the picture away. "If I wanted your opinion, I would've asked for it."

Funny, but you did ask for my opinion. "I just think you should know what you're up against."

"Yes, well. Let's leave that to my photographer. Now...can you make my girls a hat like that, or not?"

"I don't see why not. Beatrice, do we still have that green velvet from the Boudreaux's—"

"Oh no," Sabine quickly interjected, "nothing from someone else's wedding. Everything has to be brand new. I will *not* take someone else's leftovers. And, in case I haven't made myself clear, money is no object."

Crystal clear. However much I longed to say that, though, those imaginary bills kept dancing in front of my eyes.

"I understand. But, in that case, the process may take a little more time. We'll have to import all the straw. I'm glad your father has a large budget, because that much parabuntal straw could get expensive."

"My father? What does my father have to do with this? It's the bridesmaids' responsibility to pay for their outfits. Emily Post says so."

"You're right. That's the way it used to be. But not everyone follows Emily Post nowadays."

"Well, I do," she snapped. "And Emily Post says it's up to the bridesmaids to pay for their own dresses and hats."

Now, I know *Emily Post's Wedding Etiquette* backward and forward, and I could probably quote entire passages, if asked. But I also knew today's brides tended to bend the rules, if not break them altogether. And one of those rules involved who paid for the bridesmaids' clothes. Sometimes the wedding party would, but often a bride treated her friends out of the goodness of her heart.

"I just wanted you to be aware of the cost," I said. "For the sake of your friends."

"Here's the thing." Sabine slowly rose from the bar stools, apparently ready to end our conversation. "If we're going to work together, you can't question every little decision I make. To be perfectly frank…it's none of your business. Now, do we have an understanding, or don't we?"

"Of course. It's just—"

"Just nothing." Sabine clearly had tired of me. "My bridesmaids can afford your services. If they couldn't, they wouldn't be my friends in the first place."

"Okay, then." Beatrice did her best to break the tension. "Missy usually does the bride's veil first. Would you like to schedule a fitting, Miss d'Aulnay? That's normally how we kick things off."

"Certainly, but I can only meet in the afternoons. I've got doubles matches in the morning."

"No problem." Beatrice quickly slid over to the store's calendar and flipped it open. "How about Monday afternoon? Would that work for you?"

"Yes, that should be fine," Sabine said. "But we usually have brunch afterward. Can't miss that. It lasts until two."

"Two thirty it is." Beatrice quickly scribbled a note on the calendar.

"You might need these." Sabine handed me the two advertisements. "The first one's from Tiffany. Anyone can see that. The second is for some silly museum I've never heard of."

I peeked at the second ad, which featured the memorabilia from *Gone with the Wind*, including Scarlett's oversized hat. Sabine had never heard of the Louisiana Art & Science Museum? Not only did she make Stormie Lanai look like a saint—which wasn't easy—but she'd never visited one of the largest and most prestigious museums in all of Louisiana.

If ever a moment called for a "bless your heart," this was it. Too bad those blasted visions of overdue bills kept me from saying just that.

Chapter 6

The moment Sabine swooped out of Crowning Glory, I turned to Beatrice. "Gracious light! What in the world was that?"

"*That* was Sabine d'Aulnay. Her whole family's like that."

"Bless their hearts." *Whew. It feels good to finally say it.*

"Well, if you think she's bad, you should meet her mother." Beatrice rolled her eyes. "The apple didn't fall far from the tree in that family."

"Then I'm glad her momma didn't come with her to the appointment."

"She will. She will. I'll bet you anything Mrs. d'Aulnay will be at the very next one. She'll barrel through that front door and act like she's the one getting married, not one of her daughters."

"One of her daughters?" Horror tinged my voice. "You mean there's more than one?" While I'd heard about Christophe d'Aulnay through my former client, I didn't really know much about his family, like the number of daughters versus sons.

"Unfortunately, the family has five daughters. That's four more bridezillas we'll have to deal with at some point."

"Now I'm depressed." I wanted to lay my head on the counter, but I was afraid I'd fall asleep and be forced to spend the night in the studio.

"Just look at it this way. At least they pay well. That's something."

"That's the *only* thing." I straightened even more, determined to stay awake. "Did you notice something else? She didn't even bother to ask me about Hollis when I said I went out to Ruby's house today. She could've at least asked about the boy."

"Good point. That bothered me too. Speaking of which…how's Hollis holding up?"

"Not so good. We ran into someone at the house who really upset him. It was a riverboat captain by the name of Gaudet."

Recognition flickered across her face. "You must mean Remy Gaudet. He runs an airboat tour over the river."

"Well, Hollis didn't like him one bit. They almost got into a fistfight."

"A fistfight? That doesn't sound like Hollis. 'Course, I shouldn't be surprised. A lot of people around here don't like Captain Gaudet. Everyone thinks he's crooked."

"Crooked? How so?"

"They say he plays politics to keep anyone else from getting a tour operator's license."

"Do you think that's true?" While I'd run into my fair share of small-town politics with the hat studio, I didn't expect to hear politics and swamp boat tours mentioned in the same breath.

"Sure. Believe it or not, swamp tours can make a lot of money around here. It's one of the few businesses that run year-round. Of course, you have to operate more than one boat to really make the big bucks."

"Maybe that's why Hollis got so upset. He accused Captain Remy of trying to get his hands on Ruby's dock so he could run another tour."

Beatrice casually flipped the appointment book closed. "He's probably right."

"I'm just glad I got Hollis away from him. Speaking of which…" I withdrew the cell from my pocket again and checked the screen. "It's almost seven. Ambrose took Hollis back to our house. Could you lock up the studio for me? I'd like to join them."

"No problem." She slid the calendar back under the cash register. "Everything else can wait until tomorrow."

"So, there were no more disasters? Other than Sabine d'Aulnay, that is."

"Nope. Not one."

Beatrice looked confident, so I pocketed the cell and turned to leave. "Great. Thanks for locking up. I'll see you in the morning."

I made my way through the studio and stepped outside. Once I closed the door, I shuffled through the dark parking lot until I reached my Volkswagen.

The Bug waited patiently for me under the glow of an old-fashioned streetlamp, the car's paint dulled by weather and time. I'd nicknamed my Beetle Ringo when I first got it, after another—more famous—Beatle, and I loved to cruise through town with the convertible top down and a Harry Connick Jr. CD cranked up.

There was no chance of that tonight, though, since the soft breeze I'd enjoyed on the bayou had cooled once the sun set. Instead, I stepped into

Ringo and drove away from the parking lot with the ragtop locked firmly in place.

I passed several local businesses as I cruised through town, including Miss Odilia's Southern Eatery, one of my favorite restaurants, and Dippin' Donuts, another of my go-to spots. Although I had a great relationship with Odilia LaPorte, who also happened to be Lance's mother, the same couldn't be said of my relationship with the owner of Dippin' Donuts.

Grady Sebastien, who owned the bakery, had asked me out in early August, and I foolishly said yes. But only because I'd gotten into a spat with Ambrose, and I wasn't wearing a one-carat diamond engagement ring on my finger at the time.

Little did I know the rough-and-tumble baker would talk nonstop about his exploits on the Bleu Bayou High School football team throughout our one and only dinner. The guy had played football ten years ago, but he acted like it was yesterday. Not only that, but he still harbored a grudge against a teammate who'd dropped a pass in the championship game. Again...it'd happened a decade ago! I longed to leave the restaurant by the time a waitress handed us menus, and I'd completely lost my appetite halfway through the entrée. Suffice it to say, the evening was a disaster, and I still shuddered every time I drove past Grady's bakery.

The darkened windows of the donut shop scrolled past me now as I continued my trek through town. By the time I parked my Volkswagen in the driveway of the pink cottage I shared with Ambrose, I wanted nothing more than a hot meal and a good conversation with him and Hollis.

Especially if the meal involved Ambrose's jambalaya. The thought of his cooked sausage and dirty rice propelled me from the driver's seat and onto a garden path that wound around our Pepto-Bismol-pink cottage.

Uh-oh. Something's wrong.

Normally, whenever Ambrose cooked jambalaya, the spicy smells of andouille sausage and minced garlic seeped through cracks in the house's drywall. But tonight, the only smell to reach me came from some bee balm I'd planted over the garden gate. The minty scent enveloped me as I passed under the arch and approached the house. It was a light, candy-cane smell, which did nothing to stop the growl in my stomach.

I cautiously made my way to the front door, which was ajar, and spotted Ambrose and Hollis in the living room. They sat on either end of the Naugahyde couch, a Nerf football in play above their heads.

"Hey, you're back." Ambrose glanced at me as I stepped into the living room.

"Yep, I'm back. Soooo...what're you guys up to?"

"Relaxing," Ambrose said. "Hollis here was telling me about your visit to the police station today."

"Uh, that's nice." I scooted closer to the couch. Maybe I'd overlooked the smell. Just to be sure, I gave another whiff. *Nothing.* "Say, Ambrose. Weren't you going to make dinner tonight?"

"Already did." He tossed Hollis a pass without missing a beat. "Your boy here ate the whole meal cold. He didn't even wait for me to reheat it. Just scooped it cold from the pot and called it delicious."

"It's true," Hollis said. "Tasted like my granny's, as a matter of fact."

"But it's all gone?" I tried to keep my voice even. "Even Bettina's sweet rolls?"

"Yep. Even the sweet rolls." Ambrose let a pass from Hollis sail over his head when he must have realized why I was asking. "Uh-oh. You were expecting dinner tonight, weren't you?"

"Kinda." I tried not to sound miserable, but the whine came out anyway. "I thought there'd be leftovers."

"My gosh...I'm so sorry." Hollis pursed his lips. "I was really, really hungry. Please don't blame Mr. Jackson. It's all my fault."

"Don't be silly." No need to make the poor boy feel even worse than he already did. "I should've gotten something to eat on the drive home. It's not your fault. It's mine."

By now, Ambrose had straightened. "No, that's not right, Missy. We should've saved some for you. What if I take you guys out tonight? My treat."

He doesn't have to ask me twice. "Well, if you insist." I turned and retreated through the front door, relieved to hear the loud *squeak* of couch springs as Ambrose and Hollis slid off the cushions.

"Hey! Wait for us," Hollis called out. "You'll never believe what else happened today."

Chapter 7

Tired as I was, I managed to retreat down the garden path and walk to where Ambrose had parked his Audi Quattro. I waited for Hollis to hop into the car's back seat, and then I settled into the front one, next to Ambrose.

We had the whole road to ourselves as the car moved down Highway 18. Hollis told me all about finding his grandmother's sister, who was still alive, and who was still living up in Baton Rouge.

As he spoke, we drove past the old Sweetwater mansion, which sat high on a hill on the left side of the street. Shadows danced across the house's wide front porch, cast there by a single coachman's lantern that hung above a double-wide door.

There was no sign of Hank Dupre, the property's owner, or his car, which he normally parked by the kitchen window. Hank bought the mansion about a year ago, after the former owner passed away. At one point, I'd hoped to purchase the house and fix it up, but that was before I discovered a body in an outbuilding. The discovery quashed my desire to own the property once and for all, but that was yet another story for another day and time, just like the story about the kitchen garden Ruby kept outside her mobile home.

After we drove another mile or so, the outline of Dippin' Donuts, the bakery owned by Grady Sebastien, my erstwhile summer date, appeared. Like always, a neon arrow shot from the bakery's roof, and the fluorescent tube spelled out TASTY DELITES in glowing red letters.

We traveled awhile longer, until we arrived at Miss Odilia's Southern Eatery. Although we hadn't discussed where to eat, both Ambrose and I automatically headed for Miss Odilia's whenever the subject of dinner arose.

The restaurant was housed in a one-story brick cottage built just after World War I. In addition to being a wonderful cook, Miss Odilia loved to garden, and her handiwork was evident in some purple flower boxes that bookended the windows. The containers burst with fat foxglove, sky-high delphiniums, and stately calla lilies.

Ambrose pulled up alongside one of the boxes when we reached the restaurant's parking lot. I couldn't help but admire the lush blue, purple, and goldenrod buds as I left the car and made my way to the restaurant's front door.

Fortunately, Miss Odilia stood next to a hostess stand by the front door, her head bent toward a young employee who was dressed all in black.

Like always, my friend wore a starched chef's coat with a fleur-de-lis on the pocket, and she'd twisted her hair into a neat white chignon.

She dashed away from the hostess stand the moment I stepped into the building. "Shut my mouth and call me Shirley!" She swooped me up in her arms and squeezed me so hard I thought I might pop.

"Hello," I squeaked.

The chef's coat smelled like fried bread crumbs and cracked pepper, with a hint of Aqua Net hairspray thrown in.

"I'm so glad you're working at this restaurant tonight!"

"Me too," she said. "I almost worked at the other one today."

Once she made a go of her restaurant in Bleu Bayou, Miss Odilia launched a second location in New Orleans. While I cheered her success, I longed for the days when I could wander into this place and instantly find her in the kitchen.

"I just came back to town this morning. Doesn't that beat all?"

She paused when she noticed someone behind me. "Is that you, Ambrose Jackson? You get more and more handsome every day. Come on over here and let me give you some sugar!"

Ambrose dutifully stepped forward, and she released me to envelop him in a bear hug.

"Hello, Miss Odilia." His voice sounded squeaky too. "You look pretty good yourself. Are you working out?"

"Fat chance of that!" She reluctantly released him. "You always did know what to say to the ladies, though. I'm so glad you both came to my restaurant tonight."

Her words reminded me of something—or, more precisely, some*one*—else. Hollis had been standing behind us the whole time, but I almost forgot he was there because he was so quiet.

"We brought someone with us tonight. Hollis, why don't you come over here and say hello to Miss Odilia?"

Hollis hung back by the door, though, his face mired in shadows. Either he didn't hear me, or he wanted to avoid getting one of Miss Odilia's signature hugs. *Typical teenager.*

"Hollis?"

"Hey, there." Finally, he mumbled a reply.

"Come join us," I said.

"I'm okay here." His didn't budge, but his hand moved to the hem of his Lynyrd Skynyrd T-shirt, which he roughly tugged at. He seemed to think he could cover the top of his Nike shorts with the black T-shirt, if he only tugged hard enough.

"Are you okay, Hollis?" Odilia asked. "I heard all about what happened to your grandmother this morning. I'm so sorry. I'll try to bring you some casseroles as soon as I can."

"You might have to wait a week or two," I said. "Hollis is staying with us for now."

"He is? Well, that's good. I'd hate to think of someone staying out there on the bayou all alone, with no one for company but those gators."

I snuck another look at Hollis, who continued to fuss with his T-shirt. Although Miss Odilia's Southern Eatery wasn't exactly a four-star restaurant, it did offer crisp white table linens, shiny silverware, and rounded captains' chairs covered in rich leather. Was that it? Was Hollis worried about his clothes?

I leaned over to Odilia. "By any chance, do you have a spare dinner jacket in the back?" While Hollis hadn't mentioned it, his body language spoke volumes. And, at this rate, he'd rip a hole in that T-shirt if he didn't stop fiddling with it.

"As a matter of fact," Odilia said, "I do. Wait right here, and I'll run and get it."

Ambrose shot me a confused look when Odilia left our group, but I didn't bother to explain. What if Hollis overheard me? He'd only feel worse about his clothes, and that was the last thing I wanted.

"Guess she had to check something in the back," I mumbled.

We waited a few moments until she returned. She'd slung a dove-gray sports coat over one of her arms, which swayed in the air as she walked toward us.

"Ta-da!" she said, a bit breathlessly, once she reached us. "Someone left his jacket here last night, and he hasn't come back to claim it. It's a tad chilly in the dining room tonight. Why don't you wear it, Hollis?"

"That'd be great." Hollis breathed the words, obviously relieved. "I mean, only if you don't care."

"Not at all." Odilia passed him the suitcoat. "It might be a little big for you, but no one will notice."

Hollis shyly took the jacket, and then he threaded his arms through the sleeves. The coat's shoulders drooped forward, which made one of the lapels overlap the other one, but it'd have to do.

"Is that better?" I asked.

"Much," Hollis said. "It's kinda big, but that's okay. Anything's better than what I was wearing."

Now that we'd solved one problem, it was time to tackle another. "If I don't get some food in me soon, I'm going to faint dead away!"

"You poor thing," Odilia said. "Why don't you head over to the hostess stand and let Jessica find you a seat." She pointed to the girl in black. "I've gotta run back to the kitchen now, but I'll pop out for a visit when I can."

With that, Odilia bustled away, taking with her the smell of cracked pepper, fried panko, and Aqua Net hairspray. I made a beeline for the hostess stand, while Ambrose and Hollis followed.

"Hello." I approached the girl. "We'd like some dinner, please." Although I don't usually drop names, the hole in my stomach got the best of me. "We're friends of Mrs. LaPorte's."

That got the girl's attention, and she plucked three menus off the podium. "Of course. Follow me, please."

She briskly led us toward the dining room, where the low murmur of voices seeped through an open door. About two dozen tables filled the room, each dressed in a crisp linen cloth, and each ringed by a quartet of leather-backed captain's chairs. Above our heads hung heavy iron chandeliers that filled the room with a warm glow.

Unfortunately, I wasn't the only one who wanted dinner that night. Every table in the restaurant was taken, the crowd a mix of young couples, lively families, and gray-haired retirees.

I spied only one empty table in our path. It perched awkwardly in an alcove on the left, with most of the headroom taken up by two crossbeams that met in the middle. I'd eaten there once before, and I seemed to recall a near miss when I tried to rise from the table at the end of the meal and almost bonked my head on a crossbeam. I didn't exactly care to repeat that experience tonight.

But, luckily, Jessica made a sharp turn that veered us away from the alcove, and then she brought us to another table I hadn't noticed.

This one sat directly in front of a window, and it offered a panoramic view of the dining room. I couldn't believe our good fortune.

"It's perfect!" I squealed, so pleased with our luck. "Look, Ambrose, we can see everything from here."

"Glad you like it." Jessica dropped the menus on the table's edge, and then she backed away again.

I was about to repeat something about our good fortune again when I realized the reason for it. Someone had placed a Reserved sign next to a saltshaker on the table, which meant it was probably the best seat in the house.

"I feel so guilty," I told Ambrose, as he pulled out a chair for me. "She didn't have to give us such a great table."

"Look at it this way," he sat next to me, "it's impolite to look a gift horse in the mouth. Odilia would want us to sit here."

"I guess so." I turned to Hollis, who carefully tucked in his coattails before he settled into one of the other chairs. "Is this spot okay with you, Hollis?"

"It's great, actually. Granny and I never got to eat anyplace this fancy. We did go to Cracker Barrel once, but only because it was my birthday."

"That's so sweet." I leaned over and cupped my hand over his. Surprisingly, he didn't flinch, and he didn't pull his hand away. "I know you miss your grandmother. I'm so sorry about what happened today."

"Me too. I can't quite wrap my head around it. I wish she was here with us. She'd probably order one of those big ol' Bloody Marys she always liked, and then maybe some mozzarella sticks." He chuckled.

"I wish she was here too." I slowly straightened again when a waiter appeared beside us.

"Care for some rolls?" He placed a basket near my elbow.

Hallelujah and pass the ammunition. Although a dinner napkin covered the steaming rolls, the doughy smell of fresh-baked bread seeped through the open folds in the fabric. It was all I could do not to tip the basket upside down and let the rolls tumble into my mouth.

"You have to try these, Hollis." I reached for the basket. "You'll love Miss Odilia's butter rolls."

I was about to pass them to him when I remembered something. "Oh, wait," I teased. "I forgot...you've already eaten. You're probably stuffed right now."

"'Scuse me?" His eyes widened as I pulled the basket away.

"Just kidding. Here you go."

I waited for Hollis to take a roll, and then I did the same. After two or three hearty bites, I smacked my lips contentedly. "That was worth the wait."

"Always is," Ambrose said. "It always is."

"So, you come here all the time?" Hollis asked.

"We come here a lot," I said. "We like to support local places. We think it's important to give our business to our neighbors and friends."

"That's what I thought people would do with my gator farm," Hollis said. "I was hoping they'd pick me for a tour when they realized I was a local guy."

"Doesn't it usually work like that?" I asked.

Hollis shook his head. "Not always. We have people around here who say they're from the river, but they're not. Then they try to give tours, like they've been around the Atchafalaya forever. What a scam."

The scene with Hollis and Remy Gaudet immediately came to mind. He'd been so angry to find the riverboat captain on his grandmother's stretch of land.

"By any chance, are you talking about Captain Gaudet?" I asked.

"Yeah," Hollis said. "That guy's from Alabama. He tells everyone he knows the river, but I think he learned about it on YouTube."

Ambrose started to chuckle, but he stopped. "Oh, sorry. You're serious. I thought you were kidding."

"It's lying, Mr. Jackson. Plain and simple," Hollis said. "People pay good money to tour the river, and they expect their guide to be a local. He didn't even move here 'til a few years ago. It's not right, if you ask me."

"I suppose." Ambrose sobered up even more. "And I shouldn't laugh. I guess I just assumed a tour guide would have to be from around here."

"You'd think so, huh?" Hollis looked troubled now, his eyebrows knit together in a thin line. "That new mayor in town isn't even from around here."

"He's not?" I'd always assumed Zephirin Turcott, the brand-new mayor of Bleu Bayou, was a local guy. He'd recently faced the outgoing mayor in a hotly contested battle that pitted business owners against residents. Most of the business owners voted for Mayor Turcott because he promised to slice through the red tape at City Hall, while the residents voted for the outgoing mayor, who assured them Bleu Bayou had all the business it needed, thank you very much.

"Mayor Turcott isn't from around here?" I repeated. "How is that possible?"

"He moved here right before the election," Hollis said. "He's actually from Oklahoma."

"Now, how would you know that?" Hollis seemed so well versed in local politics. Most teenagers couldn't name the vice president of the United States, let alone their city's mayor.

"Easy. He came to see my grandma a few months ago. He offered her a big wad of cash if she'd sell him the house and her land."

I mulled that over. Maybe a few people had set their sights on Ruby's property. One was the person who signed the real estate contract I'd spied on Ruby's table. The other, if someone different, was Mayor Turcott.

"What did Ruby say to him?" Although I couldn't imagine she'd say yes, since most locals would never sell their property to an outsider, I wanted to hear how Hollis phrased it.

"She told him to get lost,'" Hollis said. "But he wouldn't take no for an answer. He threatened to take the property by something called em...emi—"

"You mean eminent domain?" Ambrose asked. "That's when someone takes the land by force."

"That's it!" Hollis said. "That's what he said he'd do if she didn't sell it to him."

"But isn't that usually when a city needs property for a highway or a park?" I racked my brain for some examples, since I couldn't imagine that anyone would want Ruby's property for something like that.

Somewhere along the line, probably in a prelaw class at Vanderbilt, I'd studied eminent domain. One of the more famous cases involved a Florida town and a dog park. The city council pulled the eminent domain card to get the land for it from a developer. The developer sued but he lost, so he had to pony up some of the best parcels for the proposed park. Ironically, the city council never did raise enough money to build the park, so the land sat vacant for decades.

"Politicians skirt the rules all the time," Ambrose said. "No matter what, the mayor shouldn't have threatened your grandmother like that."

We chatted a bit more about the mayor, and his unorthodox negotiation tactics, until I remembered something else. We'd completely ignored the menus on our table. While I knew what to order—since I visited Miss Odilia's place at least twice a week—Hollis wouldn't have a clue.

I passed him a menu, just as Ambrose excused himself to use the restroom.

"You might want to get the Southern Fried Chicken Deluxe platter," I offered, as I watched Ambrose walk away.

Before Hollis could respond, something hard bumped into the back of my chair. *Thwack!* I turned to see a heavyset man with a steel briefcase in his right hand. Apparently, he'd slammed the briefcase into my chair, since it swayed back and forth in the air. The stranger didn't seem to notice his faux pas until one of his dinner companions pointed it out.

"Sorry about that," he bellowed back at me. "*Pardonne-moi.*" His voice boomed above the din in the restaurant. "Guess they need to put more space between these here tables."

The man had a broad forehead and wide-set brown eyes that seemed oddly familiar. *Where have I seen that face before?*

"Yessiree," he practically yelled, "we're like sardines in a can over here. You just go right on back to your meal. Don't mind me."

The stranger wore a neon-blue camp shirt, much like Remy Gaudet's orange one, and pressed khakis. His gaze swept our table until it landed on Hollis.

"Why, Hollis Oubre. Whatever are you doing here?" he bellowed.

"Hello, Mr. d'Aulnay."

That's it! My eyes sparked when I put two and two together. The man was Sabine's father. They shared an unmistakable family resemblance— stocky build, flat nose, and dark, wide-set eyes. The elder d'Aulnay had also slicked some hair across his scalp to hide an obvious bald spot, which didn't work.

Apparently, I was about to meet the one and only Christophe d'Aulnay.

Chapter 8

Once the man finished greeting Hollis, he turned his attention to me. He didn't seem to mind being left behind by his companions, because they continued to walk through the restaurant, while he paused by our table.

He also plunked his briefcase on Ambrose's chair, as if he meant to stay awhile. "And just who might you be?"

"I'm a friend of Hollis," I said. "My name's Melissa DuBois, but everyone around here calls me Missy."

I stuck out my hand, and he grabbed it. Like his voice, his grip was a lot stronger than it needed to be.

"Nice to meet you, Missy." He pumped my hand. "Always nice to meet a pretty gal, and a redhead, to boot."

"Her fiancé's in the bathroom," Hollis quickly added. "He's a big guy. Maybe you know him. Ambrose Jackson? He's kinda famous around here."

"Jackson, huh?" The elder d'Aulnay finally released my hand, which I shook once or twice to get the blood flowing again. "Yeah, I've heard of him. Doesn't he make those girlie dresses or something?"

"It's not like that." Hollis's cheeks slowly pinked. "Yeah, he makes wedding dresses. But they cost a mint. And he's got big-time clients. Big-time. People fly him all over the country to work for them. Out of the country, even. Yeah, that's it. Europe and stuff." He limped to the end of his little speech, the wind clearly gone from his sails.

I slanted my eyes at him. While Ambrose had dressed clients from New York to California, he'd never once worked overseas, as far as I knew. With his famous followers, he didn't have to. And Hollis didn't need to lie on his behalf.

"Is that so?" Surprisingly, Christophe swallowed Hollis's story hook, line, and sinker. "Maybe I'm in the wrong business. *N'est-ce pas?*"

"Who's in the wrong business?" Ambrose had returned, although he was oblivious to the topic at hand.

"Me, apparently," Christophe said. "I had no idea your clients—"

"Good, you're back," I quickly interrupted. Maybe if I changed the subject, Ambrose wouldn't find out Hollis had lied. The boy had had enough drama for one day. "I'm guessing you two already know each other. Bo, this is Christophe d'Aulnay."

"Of course." Ambrose extended his hand, and the elder man pounced on it.

"Good to see you, son." After several hearty shakes, Christophe finally released Bo's hand. "Congratulations on your business, young man. I had no idea. But, here, let me get that briefcase out of your way. I think it's time for me to head on out, since y'all haven't eaten yet."

"We haven't even ordered yet." I glanced around our empty table. The waiter had disappeared once he dropped off the basket of rolls. Even the water glasses looked bone-dry.

"Guess our server got backed up."

"Looks like it. Maybe I should've saved you some scraps from our table." Christophe laughed heartily, and the noise cracked like thunder in the quiet space.

By now, people didn't even pretend to be interested in their own conversations as they leaned their heads toward ours. I got the funny feeling everyone expected something to happen, although I had no idea what.

"You should probably flag down the waiter," I told Ambrose, more to create a diversion than anything else. "If we don't order soon, we'll be here 'til midnight."

"Got it." Ambrose left our table again, but this time he went to find our missing server.

The minute he left, Christophe moved his briefcase to the floor so he could take Ambrose's seat. "Guess I can stay a few more minutes, then."

"But aren't your friends going to miss you?" I asked.

"Nah. I took care of the bill, so they owe me. They'll wait." He studied my face for several seconds. "Now, your name sounds familiar. Are you part of the DuBois clan out of Lafayette?"

"No, sir." Little did he know my family tree grew to the Texas border, and then the roots petered out. "I grew up in Texas, and then I went to school in Tennessee."

"A Vanderbilt girl, huh?" He studied me a moment longer. "I've got it!" Even his finger snap was loud. "That's the name of the hatmaker in town. *La modiste.* Are you any relation to her?"

"As a matter of fact, I am." A deep rumble worked its way through my stomach, but I did my best to ignore the hunger pains. "I own the hat studio. It's called Crowning Glory, and I started it up about two years ago. I work with brides and bridesmaids all up and down the Great River Road."

"I knew it." His eyes lit up. "You're the little lady who's helping my Sabine with her wedding veil."

"Yes, sir. As a matter of fact, I am."

"Now, don't go giving her any crazy ideas," he said. "My little girl tends to go a bit overboard."

Well, that ship's already sailed. But there was no need to tell him that. "All brides have a lot of fancy ideas when they first start out." I tried to be as diplomatic as possible. "My job is to take their fantasies and turn them into something real."

"That right? Well, let me give you a little tip." He leaned closer, as if I couldn't hear him well enough. "Only listen to about half of what she says. That girl thinks money grows on trees."

I subtly leaned away, since I wasn't used to someone yelling in my ear. "You don't say. Well, we'll do the best we can with the budget."

"Yep, she thinks my bank account is a bottomless pit. Truth be told, it's been a tough year so far."

"Really?" I couldn't imagine that was true, after everything Sabine had said.

"Well, there's only so much you can do—"

At that moment, Ambrose reappeared at our table with our waiter—who looked a little sheepish, to be honest—in tow. Maybe now I could quiet the grumble in my stomach.

Both Hollis and I quickly gave him our orders, and then Ambrose settled into the only chair left at the table.

"We interrupted you," I told Christophe. "You were about to say something about your business."

He'd piqued my curiosity with his claim about a tough year since it didn't jibe with Sabine's bragging.

"What's that? Oh yeah. Business." He glanced at Ambrose. "I own a little riverboat out on the Atchafalaya. It's called the *Riverboat Queen.* Maybe you've heard of it?"

"Of course," Ambrose said. "Your boat's pretty famous around here. All of my clients want to get married there."

"So, you've seen her, huh? She's a beauty, all right. My pride and joy. Used to be I could run her up and down the river all year long. But the water levels aren't the same anymore."

I cocked my head. According to Beatrice, plenty of people had made money off the swamps around here, precisely because the industry could run year-round. "Someone once told me swamp tours operate twelve months a year out here. Isn't that true?"

"Not anymore. Not since the water levels went down. *C'est la vie.*"

By this time, Hollis had completely disappeared from our conversation, so I quickly glanced at him. He looked sullen, and he'd sunk so low into the dinner jacket, his chin grazed the lapels.

What's bothering him?

"So you see, there's a catch." Christophe didn't seem to notice Hollis was hiding in the collar of his coat. "You're fine once you get to open water, but when the river dips too low, it's hard to navigate around the driftwood and such. Near impossible by August. The key is to keep boats at several spots. Give yourself some options, depending on what the river's doing that week."

Hollis finally moved, and his mouth peeked out from the collar of the coat. "You don't say."

"Why, Hollis, you should know that better than anyone else," Christophe replied. "You've lived on that riverbank your whole life. Surely you've noticed the water levels aren't up to par."

"Yeah, but that doesn't give people the right to start nosing around for other docks to steal." He threw the captain a look I couldn't quite decipher.

"I wouldn't call it 'nosing around' when I visited your grandmother, son." He emphasized the last word, as if he wanted to put Hollis in his place. "We had to talk business, that's all."

"Business? Is that what you called it?" Hollis said. "My grandma was pretty upset once you left."

Christophe laughed again, only this time it was tame compared to his first one. "I was probably teasing her about something and she took it the wrong way. Of course, I would've given her a fair price. More than fair. It's the way I do business around here. Ask anyone."

Ambrose leaned in to Hollis, as if he wanted to protect him. "What exactly did your grandmother say, Hollis?"

"Just that she supposed Mr. d'Aulnay here would find a way to get his hands on our property one way or another. And he didn't much care how he did it."

That quickly sobered up our guest. "Now, Hollis, you've gotta stop spreading rumors like that. Everyone knows I do business fair and square. Like I said, I probably made a joke and your grandma took it the wrong way."

Our guest slowly rose from the table. "Well, it's getting late, and I should probably go find my buddies. By the way"—he leaned over to grab his briefcase off the floor—"I'd still like to talk to you about that property when all the dust settles, Hollis. It's a lot of land for a kid to handle. You might want someone to take it off your hands."

Hollis started to protest, but Ambrose held him back.

"It's *wwwaaayyy* too early for that," Ambrose said. "We've got a funeral to plan first."

The riverboat captain grunted, but he didn't seem chastised by the reply. Instead, he quickly turned to leave, dragging with him the gaze of every diner within earshot. By now, silence engulfed our little corner of the restaurant and even the *clink* of silverware had dimmed.

All the attention bothered me, so I leaned close to Hollis before I spoke.

"Well, that was nervy," I whispered. "No wonder your grandmother thought he was intimidating. Heck, I thought he was intimidating, and I've only just met him."

"That guy makes me so mad." Unlike me, Hollis didn't bother to lower his voice. "He thinks he can do anything he wants, just because he's a d'Aulnay."

"Try to forget about it," I urged. "He's not important right now. Let's enjoy our meal and head on back to the house. We've all had a long day."

Which was an understatement. Once I finished dinner, I fully intended to take a hot bath and go straight to bed. Maybe then I could put this day behind me. I only hoped the universe would finally agree with my plan and let me put this day to rest.

Chapter 9

By the time I woke up the next morning, bright sunshine washed over the windowsill in my bedroom. I'd planned to get up early, but I'd forgotten to set my alarm with all the hubbub of the night before.

Who knew I'd meet Christophe d'Aulnay at Miss Odilia's restaurant? Everything I'd ever heard about the man was true: the outsized personality, the condescending tone, the way he sucked up all the oxygen in a room, just like his daughter did. The apple definitely didn't fall far from the tree in that family.

I yawned before I threw back the covers and hopped onto the cold floorboards. There was no time for breakfast today. I barely had time to change into some work clothes and maybe grab a few minutes in front of the bathroom mirror, let alone toast a bagel, scramble an egg, or cook a bowl of oatmeal.

I didn't even bother to throw on a robe as I walked down the hall, since Ambrose always left the house well before sun up—not that he'd care, anyway—and Hollis would probably sleep until noon, if yesterday was any indication. Sure enough, the *thwap* of my bare feet on the floor made the only sound as I headed for the bathroom at the end of the hall.

Just fifteen minutes in front of the mirror and I felt like a brand-new person. Afterward, I quickly threw on a lightweight wool skirt and a silky emerald top, and then I headed for the front door. I remembered to grab an umbrella from our hat stand at the very last minute, since October could bring unexpected rain showers to this part of Louisiana, and I didn't want to get caught unaware.

Once I hopped into my car, I drove onto Highway 18, one of the few cars on the road so late in the morning. I was about to enter the parking lot at the Factory when my cell buzzed. *Uh-oh.* Nothing like getting thrown into the fire before I even walked into the studio.

Only…it wasn't Beatrice's name that appeared on my cell phone. It was Lance's. By the time I pulled off to the side of the road, the buzzing stopped, but I tapped the screen and the phone quickly connected me to the police station. Like always, Lance answered my call right away.

"Hey, Missy." He sounded wide awake, since he normally arrived at the police station by six in the morning. "Are you at work yet?"

"I wish. I accidentally slept in. What's up?" Since Lance and I grew up together, we could dispense with the niceties and get right to the heart of the matter.

"Got the ME's preliminary report on Ruby last night. Thought you might be interested in it."

"You're kidding. That sure was fast."

"It has to be," Lance said. "Whenever you've got a drowning victim, they fast-track it. Otherwise, air will destroy the evidence on a corpse."

"Ewww…that's a pretty gruesome fact to wake up to. Remember, I just got up." I shook my head to clear it. "So, what'd the ME find?"

"Look, I can't talk about this over the phone. Any chance you can head on over here to the police station?"

"I don't know." I could only imagine how much work waited for me when I got to the studio. Since I'd spent most of the day before on the bayou with Hollis, countless e-mails no doubt clogged my in-box, and a stack of telephone messages probably spewed across my drafting table.

"The report is short, Missy. Short, and very surprising."

"Surprising, huh? You're killing me, Lance." He always did know what to say to make me do something I didn't want to do. Even when we were little kids, he knew what buttons to push until I agreed to help him with one of his schemes. The more things changed…

"It's your call," he said.

"All right. All right. I'll be there in five. But I expect some coffee when I get to your place. The good stuff too. Not that sludge you usually make."

"You got it. I'll make you a pot of Community coffee."

With that, Lance clicked off the line, and I did the same. After making a quick U-turn, I drove for five minutes or so, until the police substation came into view.

Traffic was light on this road too, probably because the weekend wouldn't kick off until tonight, when everyone got off work at five. That was when the streets would come alive and people sloughed off the memory of the workweek by visiting one of their favorite watering holes. Although Bleu

Bayou was a far cry from New Orleans crime-wise, we still had our fair share of DUIs, domestic violence calls, and whatnot. One time I even watched the police bust up a fistfight at Antoine's Country Kitchen, only to nab a purse snatcher on their way out the door. Such was life in a small town when there were big cities nearby.

But today was different. Today I had the whole road to myself, and then I had my choice of parking spaces once I reached the police station. I pulled Ringo into the first row, next to an unmarked squad car. Lance's Oldsmobile was nowhere to be found, which meant he must've left it at home. Although I liked to tease him about his grimy Buick, it was probably for the best, since it wasn't exactly the best advertisement for a police department. Better for him to borrow a shiny new squad car and leave the clunker at home.

I skirted around the hood of the unmarked car and entered the station through a plate-glass door. Lance stood behind a counter that reached his waist. It separated the lobby from the rest of the room. Everything from the filing cabinets to my right and the windowsills behind me to the ceiling tiles overhead had been slathered with gray paint. Either they had a paint sale at Homestyle Hardware, or the maintenance person lacked imagination.

In contrast, Lance wore a spit-and-polish navy-blue police uniform, complete with gold piping and epaulets on the shoulders. The epaulets were a tad much, in my opinion, but he *did* look official in the regulation garb.

"My, my," I said, as soon as I caught his eye. "Don't you look snazzy."

He smirked as he reached for a button that was hidden beneath the counter. One *pop* and a gate swung open, which allowed me to enter the area where the police officers sat.

"Long time, no see." I quickly walked over to where he stood. Although he'd joined me on the banks of the Atchafalaya River only the day before, it felt like a lifetime had passed. I remembered watching a police diver telescope the snag pole that he'd use to catch Ruby's clothing under the water; the way the doors to the coroner's van stood wide open, inviting anyone to get an eyeful of the contents inside; and the drive back to Ruby's house, when Hollis fell asleep on my shoulder before we even got to the property.

"Let's go back to my desk." Lance motioned me to an area near the far wall.

I followed him past a half-dozen tidy work spaces, decorated with plastic photo frames, neatly organized files, and coffee mugs imprinted with WORLD'S BEST MOM or #1 GRANDDAD. Then we got to Lance's desk.

Heaven help us. Unlike the rest of the workstations, Lance's desk groaned under the weight of file folders, fat notebooks, and whatnot. I half-expected the table to crumble under the weight of the debris right then and there.

At least the chair he pulled out for me was clean, so I quickly sat. "Hmph."

"What's wrong?" he asked.

"There could be a family of racoons living under all that paper, Lance. How can you even find anything?"

"Very funny." As if to prove me wrong, Lance plunged his hand into the pile and yanked out a black folder decorated with a seal for the St. James Parish Coroner's Office. The foil seal winked at me as he waved it in the air. "Aha! Right where I put it."

I gave him my signature eye roll. "Bravo."

"And now, for my next trick..." He smiled before he handed me the black folder. "Just kidding. Here you go."

I cautiously took the folder, since I knew the drill by now. Ever since I helped Lance solve a murder at Morningside Plantation, some two years ago, I'd read more than my fair share of coroners' reports and medical examiners' notes.

According to Lance, he always included me in his police investigations because I possessed an unusually fine-tuned intuition. Although sometimes I wondered whether it was because he trusted me, seeing we were knee-babies together back in Texas. Either way, we'd successfully solved three other cases before this one, so who was to say he was wrong?

"It's only two pages for now," Lance said. "Just the preliminary. But the ME got suspicious when he saw the victim's hands."

"Her hands?" I flipped open the cover to see a typewritten page awash in black ink.

"When people drown, they usually clench their hands, because they're trying to fight to get to the surface. But that didn't happen here. Sometimes the ME will even see bruised muscles from the struggle."

"Well, that doesn't make sense. Someone strong, like Ruby, would fight like crazy to get out of the water."

"Bingo. And we know she wasn't killed on land, because she'd curled up in a semi-fetal position under the water. That meant she was alive when water filled her lungs."

I crinkled my nose. "I'm not following you. If she didn't die on land, and she didn't fight to get to the surface, what happened?"

"C'mon, Missy. You're not thinking. There's another possibility. What if she couldn't fight? What if someone drugged her?"

"If that's the case, then the ME would've found drugs in her system, right?"

"True. But this is just a preliminary report, so it doesn't have the results of a full drug panel. That'll take about a week to get back. But the ME did get lucky in this case. He suspected a 'knockout drug.' Something that relaxes the muscles quickly. The most popular drugs are Xanax and something called lorazepam. They act fast, and you can't smell them. Criminals love those drugs because they don't make people nauseous, so their victims never realize what's happening to them."

"That's diabolical." I shuddered, and it had nothing to do with the freezing air-conditioning. "And that's what the ME found in her system?"

"Yep. The lab did a quick blood analysis and it came back positive. Now, will they find other drugs in her system? Maybe. But those are the ones he zeroed in on because they made the most sense."

"I'll be darned." It sounded like something from a Hollywood movie, or maybe a news story ripped from the pages of the *Times-Picayune* in New Orleans. Used to be that kind of thing would never happen in Bleu Bayou, although I couldn't say that anymore.

"You can read the report for yourself." Lance nodded at the pages in my hand. "It won't take you long."

"Okay. And I've got a great idea. How about some of that coffee you promised, so I can focus on the report?"

"You got it."

While Lance left to fill a Styrofoam coffee cup for me, I glanced at the first page in my hand. It was simple enough to follow. First came a basic checklist under the heading Information About the Decedent, which captured routine stats, like the victim's marital status, eye color, and weight. Next came a space for information about the incident. Did the victim die in someone's home? A swimming pool? That sort of thing.

I noticed a bold red checkmark in the next section, which asked for the manner of death. Given the choice of natural, homicide, accident, suicide, undetermined, or pending, the ME had chosen the very last option.

Wonder why he didn't just label it a homicide?

By now Lance had returned to his desk with a steaming cup of coffee, which I gratefully accepted. Since I couldn't find a clean spot for it on the desk, I carefully balanced the cup on the chair's armrest.

"Say, Lance. Why didn't the ME just call it a homicide, since the test for the knockout drug came back positive?"

"Because he wanted to keep his options open. By calling the ruling 'pending,' he'll get an autopsy, but he doesn't have to make a final determination until all the results come back."

"Gotcha." I once more dropped my gaze to the report. Another section bore the title Means of Death—If Other Than Natural, and it included a subsection on drugs. Here, someone had scrawled a handwritten note:

In the absence of full blood or urine panels, suspected Xanax/lorazepam discovered in bloodstream and gastric contents.

I finally glanced away. "Okay, so tell me a little bit about this knockout drug. I've never heard of it before."

"You've probably heard of it. You just didn't realize it at the time. It's used in a lot of sexual assaults. Say a woman goes to a bar and accepts a drink from a guy she doesn't know. He slips the knockout drug into it when she's not looking, and bingo...she's out cold and he can do anything he wants."

"You're not saying..."

"No, no. Ruby wasn't assaulted that way," Lance said. "But she was given enough of the drug to render her unconscious. Like I said, it doesn't have any odor or color, so her assailant could've mixed it with anything. Something as simple as that cup of coffee you have."

I glanced at the Community coffee steaming away at my elbow. Given the timing—Beatrice and I had arrived at the bayou yesterday morning—it all made perfect sense.

"What're you going to do next?" I carefully returned the report to Lance before I lifted the coffee and slowly took a sip.

"Gotta round up the suspects. We all know Ruby was sitting on a prime piece of property out there on the river. Maybe someone killed her for the land."

"I agree. I saw a real estate letter sitting on Ruby's cocktail table. It looked like someone offered to buy her property before she died."

"Did you leave it alone?"

"Of course." I gave him my signature eye roll, since I knew better than to disturb a crime scene by now.

"Good," Lance said. "Plus, what if Ruby found out something in one of her jobs she wasn't supposed to know? After all, she worked for some powerful people back in her day."

"Interesting."

Ruby had served as a caretaker for several mansions before she retired. Her bosses included Herbert Solomon, a wealthy billionaire out of Baton Rouge, and Hank Dupre, who purchased the Sweetwater mansion a few years back. But Mr. Solomon died in August, and Hank was trustworthy to a fault. Could she have crossed someone else along the way?

"That's why I want you to keep your eyes and ears open," Lance continued. "Especially around Hollis. He might've heard something important without even realizing it."

"He's staying at my house right now, so I can talk to him anytime I want. He was still sleeping when I left for work this morning." I quickly glanced at a bald-faced clock over Lance's desk. "Yikes! It's already nine. If I don't get to work soon, Beatrice's going to send out a search party. I've gotta run, but I'll call you soon."

I hurried away from Lance's desk, with one eye on the ticking clock.

Thankfully, traffic remained light on Highway 18 as I made my way toward Crowning Glory. Only a few Marathon Oil tankers dotted the road, and even those would turn off after only an exit or two.

All was well until I approached the parking lot at the Factory and found it stuffed to the gills with delivery vans, SUVs, and fancy sedans. *Sweet mother of pearl!*

The vehicles sat cheek-by-jowl on the asphalt, their owners long since swallowed up by the Factory's studios. After cruising around the lot three times, and cursing my bad luck on each go-round, I finally spotted a place in the very last row, sandwiched between an enormous Lexus SUV and a telephone pole. I swerved into the tight space and dashed from my car, ducking around chrome bumpers, extra-long side panels, and sloped hoods on my way to the studio.

Once I arrived at Crowning Glory, I threw open the door and braced myself for the chaos I'd surely find inside.

"I'm back!" I yelped, as I skipped over the welcome mat.

"Hey, there."

Contrary to my opinion, Beatrice languidly perched on a bar stool in front of our counter, and she barely turned her head to acknowledge me. Her uncle Hank sat beside her, and they both had fresh Starbucks coffees. Obviously, I'd interrupted a family chitchat, and not a full-blown crisis, like I'd expected.

"Good morning, Missy," Hank said, as I scurried across the room.

"Good morning. Sorry I'm so late! I had to stop by the police station—"

"Whoa. Slow down." He immediately rose from his chair. "Here. Take my seat. We were just chatting about this and that."

"That's okay. I'm fine." I waved away his offer, nice as it was. "It's good to see you, Mr. Dupre, but I've got a gazillion things to do around here."

"Missy."

The minute he cocked an eyebrow, I realized my mistake. "I'm sorry. I meant to call you Hank." How many times did the poor guy have to remind me? For some reason, I never could use his first name. Maybe it was his age—he was at least twenty years older—or his senatorial demeanor, but his first name stuck in my throat whenever I tried to use it.

"That's better." He nodded briskly. "One of these days I'm going to strike that 'Mr. Dupre' stuff right out of your vocabulary."

"And you don't have to rush around," Beatrice added. "Things are pretty calm right now. Sabine d'Aulnay called a few minutes ago to say she wants to come back to the studio this morning. But she won't get here until around nine thirty, so we have plenty of time."

"Huh. What a coincidence. I ran into Sabine's father last night at dinner."

"You ran into Christophe d'Aulnay?" Hank looked amused. "Let me guess...he talked your ear off in that loud voice of his."

"Sure enough," I said. "Doesn't he realize he could wake the dead with it?"

"Of course, he does," Hank replied. "He does it on purpose. He's like a dog that wants to mark its territory and let everyone know he was there."

"Uncle." Beatrice shot him a stern look. "That's not very nice. You're always telling me I shouldn't say something if it's not nice."

"That's only for normal people. It doesn't apply to someone like Christophe d'Aulnay. Then you can go ahead and be as mean as you want."

Now that things had turned interesting, I debated whether to take that empty chair after all. Although I had a million things to do this morning and only a few hours to get them done, Hank's comment had piqued my curiosity, so I slid onto the bar stool. "Why don't you like Christophe d'Aulnay?"

"Because he thinks he walks on water. They all do. I wouldn't be surprised if one day Christophe tries to get our mayor to change the name of Bleu Bayou to d'Aulnay Bayou."

"C'mon, Uncle." Beatrice shot him another look. "He's not that bad."

"You've said it yourself about the family." Hank playfully elbowed her in the side. "I don't see you hanging around with any of his daughters."

"Ugh. I have to side with Beatrice on that one," I said. "I've met his firstborn. But, listen. I interrupted you two, and your coffees are getting cold. Don't let me get in the way of your conversation."

"It's okay," Hank said. "We were just talking about what happened yesterday. That's the big topic around here."

Beatrice tilted her cup at me, but I shook my head at the offer. One cup of coffee with Lance was more than enough for now. Otherwise, I'd be bouncing off the walls by the time Sabine showed up at my studio.

"What was it like on the river yesterday?" Hank asked.

"It wasn't pleasant," I said. "It still rattles me. It felt like we spent a week out there, and not just a few hours."

The scene seemed surreal, even now. The way daylight had glinted off the water like shards of glass. The muddy knob that protruded from a blanket of emerald hydrilla. The look on Hollis's face when he came up for air with his grandmother's clog in his right hand.

"Hollis was the one who found her body," I said.

"We know," Beatrice said. "I can't imagine finding your grandmother's body like that. I'm so glad you took him in, Missy."

"You heard about that too, huh? He didn't have anywhere else to go. When that smarmy Remy Gaudet showed up at the property, I knew Hollis couldn't stay there overnight. Heck, the two of them almost clobbered each other, and I was standing right there."

"Remy Gaudet?" Hank said. "I didn't know he went out to Ruby's house yesterday. I told him to stay away from that property. He obviously didn't listen to me."

"You what?" Maybe I needed that second cup of coffee after all, because I didn't understand what he was saying.

"Remy asked me to draft a letter of intent for Ruby's property, which I did," Hank said. "But I counseled him to stay away from Ruby. He's another one who comes off as a bit strong, and I didn't want Ruby to bolt before she had a chance to read the letter."

"I can see why you'd do that. He basically trespassed onto the property yesterday afternoon. We caught him right in the middle of measuring the dock. Which was pretty nervy, because he had to know Hollis would return to the house at some point."

"Maybe he didn't care," Beatrice said.

"Maybe." I remembered the way the swamp guide accused me of sneaking up on him. As if I was in the wrong. "The funny thing is, he never apologized to Hollis. He acted like it was our fault for not welcoming him with open arms."

"That's Remy, all right," Hank said. "He's a legend in his own mind too. Sorry you and Hollis had to run into him like that. There must be something in the river water that makes those guys act so crazy. Both Remy and Christophe think they own the Atchafalaya."

"It's true," Beatrice agreed. "And what they don't own, they're trying to get their hands on."

Something clicked just then. I'd spied the letter of intent when I straightened the newspapers in Ruby's home and wondered why she'd stashed it between the front section of the *Bleu Bayou Impartial Reporter* and the want ads. It didn't seem like the best place to keep an important document if she wanted to sell the property.

"To be honest, I'm not sure Ruby took the letter of intent very seriously," I said. "She stored it with the old newspapers, like it was trash or something."

"Hmmm. Really?" He paused to consider it. "Then again, I can't say I'm too surprised. Ruby never liked formalities. She'd rather shake hands than sign a document. That's how they do things out on the river."

"Did she ever answer you?" I asked.

"No, not really. And to tell you the truth, it worried me. Especially since—"

At that moment, the door to my studio burst open. Hank's voice trailed off as we all turned to acknowledge the sound.

Of all the times for a client to rush into the studio, why did it have to be now?

Chapter 10

"*Bonjour*, people. *Bonjour.*" Sabine d'Aulnay bustled into the room, her coat a red blur against all the white on the display tables.

Today she wore an expensive St. John suit with tufted cuffs and collar, and she carried an oversized Louis Vuitton satchel in the exact same shade of red.

It was hard to know where to look first…at the over-the-top suit, which featured dozens of tiny safety pins stabbed into the hem, or at her eyes, which bore into mine as she rushed up to the counter.

"I know I'm early," she breezed, "but I was in the neighborhood, and I hate to waste time. Thought I might as well stop in for my appointment."

She didn't bother to acknowledge either Beatrice or Hank.

"Good morning." I spoke slowly, hoping to stall her pace a little. "It's nice to see you."

"Of course it is." She plunked her enormous handbag on the counter, which nearly toppled Beatrice's coffee cup. "I need to talk to you about my veil."

"I see." I made a point of acknowledging Hank first. "I take it you've met Mr. Dupre? He's a local Realtor, and he owns the old Sweetwater mansion."

"Yes, yes. Of course." She gave him a cursory nod. "Now, about my order—"

"And you met Beatrice yesterday," I said brightly, not the least bit concerned about the way her eyes narrowed. Although I wanted to stay on Sabine's good side, since she was paying for my services, that didn't mean I had to suffer her rudeness in silence.

"Yes, yes. How are you?" She didn't wait for Beatrice to respond. "I'd like to get ahold of that sketch you're working on. The one for my veil."

"But we only spoke about it yesterday." Surely she didn't expect me to have a full design finished by now. Even *she* couldn't be that demanding. Could she?

"I know, but something came up, and I want to show it to my father. If you don't have a drawing ready, at least give me the Tiffany ad back."

"Of course. I put it in my workroom."

"Looks like you two ladies have business to conduct." Hank slowly moved away from us, as gallant as ever, despite the snub by Sabine. "I'll call you later, Beatrice."

"Hold up, Uncle Hank." Since she'd spotted a chance to make a clean getaway, Beatrice seized it. "You forgot your Starbucks." She grabbed the cup and leapt off the stool, her footwork surprisingly fast for someone who'd lounged at the counter only a moment before.

"But..." My voice faltered as Beatrice disappeared through the exit. Although I couldn't blame her for wanting to get away from Sabine, I didn't relish the thought of being left alone with our newest bridezilla.

"That's okay." Sabine sniffed dismissively. "We don't need them anyway."

"Why don't you make yourself comfortable, and I'll go grab the ad." I tried to sound as agreeable as possible. "It'll only take me a second."

I hurried to the workroom to retrieve the page. Before I returned to the studio, though, I quickly grabbed a pen from my drafting table and scribbled the phone number for Crowning Glory in the upper right-hand corner. That would make it easy for Sabine to get in touch with me afterward.

When I reentered the studio, I spied the girl by a display table near the front door. She held a riding crop in her right hand, which she swished against her thigh. The whip served as a prop for a display I'd created that focused on outdoor weddings.

Thwack! After slapping her thigh one last time, she finally noticed me. "Why in the world do you keep this here?"

"Because it goes with the white top hat and kid gloves. It's a whole equestrian theme."

"How...clever." She carelessly tossed the crop back on another table, where it landed with a *thud*. "Seems kind of silly, though. Anyone who rides will know that's a driving whip. You should've used a dressage whip, which is a lot fancier."

"Trust me, I know all about whips." By now, she'd worn my patience thinner than the mother-of-pearl veneer on the crop's handle. "I learned all about horseback riding when I was in college."

Like any good Vanderbilt girl, I attended the Kentucky Derby every year, and I'd designed oodles of Derby hats for my sorority sisters. Those experiences taught me everything I needed to know about riding, including what crops to use for different events. "I chose a driving whip because I wanted a long lash for the display. The handle on a dressage whip is much too short."

"*Hmph.* I guess you do know." She seemed surprised but determined not to show it. "Anyway, thanks for getting me the ad. I'd like to show it to my dad."

"No problem." I gingerly handed over the magazine clip. "I can probably come up with a design for your veil by next week. I'll work on it over the weekend."

"Why don't you hold off." She accepted the paper just as gingerly as I'd proffered it. "Let's see what my father says first. He might want me to go in a different direction, and I wouldn't want you to waste your time."

"You're the client. Just let me know what he says."

She pulled a cell from the pocket of her pricey suit and checked its screen. "I've got to get going. Planning a wedding takes *soooo* much work." She grabbed her satchel and twirled away from me, the oversized bag nearly grazing my elbow.

"Should I wait for your call, then?" I called out, as she moved through the studio.

"Fine. Whatever. *Au revoir!*"

"Good-bye."

An uneasy feeling washed over me the moment she stepped through the exit. She couldn't wait to get her hands on the Tiffany ad, and then she abruptly left. Not only that, but why did she want to show her father a picture of someone else's veil—albeit a beautiful one with oodles of sparkly diamonds—when most fathers didn't even see a wedding dress, let alone a veil, before the big day? Surely Christophe d'Aulnay had more important things to worry about, like his most recent business woes.

"Is she gone?" Beatrice peeked around the front door a few moments later.

"Yep, she's gone. She just left."

"Whew! I thought I'd have to spend time with her for sure." Beatrice gingerly stepped over the welcome mat, as if she didn't quite believe me. "But as long as she's not coming back…"

"No, she's not coming back. She hightailed it out of here as soon as I gave her the ad."

"That was a little strange." Beatrice began to cross the floor, but she stopped short of the display table with the equestrian theme. "And what happened here? Something's missing."

"That was Sabine's handiwork. She tossed the riding crop on another table when she was done playing with it. And I agree with you. I can't imagine why she'd want to show the ad to her father."

"Look on the bright side." Beatrice snatched the crop from the wrong table and returned it to its rightful place. "The day can only go up from here."

"Agreed. So, what's on your plate today?"

"I thought I'd do that inventory report you asked me about. We don't have any more appointments this morning, so I can check out the storage closet."

"That's right. I forgot all about that." Between the hubbub with Ruby's passing, not to mention the surprise appearance of Sabine d'Aulnay, I'd forgotten all about the routine chores that still needed attention, like the inventory report.

We reordered our supplies every October, at the close of the wedding season. By then, the storage closet looked like a windswept prairie after a tornado, completely bare and sprinkled with dust. Oh, there might be a few bolts of Belgian lace left, or a cupful of Swarovski crystals, or maybe a flattened tube of PVA glue, but that was about it.

It wasn't due to a lack of planning. We started off strong every May, with enough supplies to get us through the busy summer months. But then the unexpected always showed up on our doorstep, right in the middle of the wedding season. Two years ago, it was a fashion show, which completely wiped out the shop's supply of taffeta, bobby pins, and dress tape, while last summer's surprise involved a wedding with twenty-four bridesmaids and twenty-four elaborate fascinators. Our stock of seed pearls never did recover after that.

"Thanks for reminding me about the inventory," I said. "And I've to get some new hat stands for a display I've been thinking about."

"Gotcha. I'll start a list."

While Beatrice moved behind the counter, I headed for the workroom out back. It was time to tackle my own projects for the day.

First up was a one-of-a-kind fascinator for a second-time bride. The client planned to hold a destination wedding in the Caribbean, and she'd requested something with a tropical vibe. Silk flowers, maybe? Come to think of it, I could craft hibiscuses out of silk and attach them to a cap of French needlepoint lace.

The trick was to find the right fabric stiffener. I headed for my recipe box, which I kept in a bookcase behind the drafting table. My fingers flew past recipes for fabric dyes, feather curlers, and permanent glues until I arrived at one for fabric stiffener. This particular recipe came courtesy of a French milliner who hired me to work at her atelier one summer.

Silk Flower Stiffener

1. Bring 14 ounces water to a boil.
2. Mix 4 tsp cornstarch with 4 tsp water to create a thin paste.
3. Pour paste into boiling water.
4. Keep stirring until the mixture boils & thickens.
5. Trickle in 8 tsp PVA glue and stir until all are combined.
6. Pour into a glass bottle and cool. Voilà!

Once I brought some water to boil on a hot plate and added the cornstarch and glue, I poured the mixture into an old Coke bottle I kept just for that purpose. Then I set about cutting the petals for my hibiscuses, a painstaking process that involved needlepoint scissors and a steady hand.

I was right in the middle of fashioning the very last flower when Beatrice walked into the workroom.

"*Ooohhh.*" She stood in front of a corkboard I'd fashioned into a holder for the finished product. A dozen flowers filled holes I'd drilled into the board. "Those flowers are beautiful! They look like they came from someone's garden."

"Wait until they dry. The silk will lighten up and get all shiny."

"I'm sorry to interrupt you," she said, "but it's lunchtime. I thought we'd get something to eat."

I paused, torn by the offer, since I only had two more flowers to go. Maybe Beatrice was right, though. I counted on her to drag me away from the drafting table whenever I got too caught up in my work. Otherwise, I tended to skip meals, which wasn't good for my health, as everyone was quick to remind me.

I quickly glanced at my cell, which I'd stashed on a far corner of the table, safely away from the glue. Two whole hours had passed since I first entered the workroom. "I had no idea it was so late! Guess time got away from me. No wonder my head hurts. I haven't had a thing to eat today."

"Missy." She gave me the same look Ambrose always used when he didn't approve of my carelessness. "You've got to eat something. Plus, you've been breathing glue fumes all morning." She leaned over the flower in my hand and inhaled. "*Pee-yew.* That stuff can't be good for you."

"I opened a window." I tried not to sound defensive, but it wasn't easy. "You don't have to act like I'm two years old. But you're right about lunch. Why don't we head into town? My treat." I held up my glue-smeared hand. "Once I clean up, that is."

"Sounds good. I'll forward our calls to my cell and turn around the welcome sign in the window."

While Beatrice left to close the shop, I headed for a sink across the way. It took three passes with Palmolive soap and a washcloth, but I finally removed the goop from my fingers. Afterward, I returned to the studio, where I found Beatrice waiting for me by the front door. She quickly extinguished the overheads when I arrived, and darkness engulfed the studio.

The parking lot seemed especially bright after that, with shards of sunshine that careened off the windshields and into my eyes. Noise abounded—tires crunching against pebbly tar, horns blaring as people tried to form a makeshift line by the exit, and country music coming from a pickup somewhere up ahead.

Once we hopped into Ringo, my VW, I patiently joined a bottleneck that formed by the exit. Before long, I steered onto Highway 18.

The saw-toothed outline of the Factory gradually disappeared from the rearview mirror as we traveled farther down the road.

"Why don't we go to Miss Odilia's place?" Beatrice watched the scenery pass by.

"I don't know. I've been eating there a lot lately. I mean, a *whole* lot."

"You could always order something different," she said. "You know, she makes more than fried chicken and butter biscuits."

"Bite your tongue! Her drumsticks trump anyone else's, and her biscuits melt in your mouth. But maybe you're right. I could go crazy and order a salad today."

The decision made, I steered the car toward Miss Odilia's Southern Eatery. Before long, a trio of pre–World War II bungalows painted in cotton-candy colors appeared on the right, which meant the restaurant was nearby.

The owners had converted the prewar houses into different shops. Glamour Girls' Nails came first, followed by Patsy's Puppy Palace, which featured paw prints on the window shades. The third bungalow housed the Kut N' Kurl, where Louella Caouette provided fancy updos, blond highlights, and the like.

Louella's place shared a wall with Uncle Billy's Self-Storage, which was a business I'd recently visited.

It happened a few months back, when I helped a construction worker load architectural elements into a unit there. At the time, I thought maybe the man stole the corbels, shutters, and whatnot, since several featured the distinctive crest of Dogwood Manor on the wood.

But that was yet another story for another time and place.

I cast one last glance through the passenger window as we moved past the pastel bungalows. Oddly enough, tan butcher paper covered the window of the Kut N' Kurl, and someone had tried to scrape off a pair of scissors painted onto the front door.

"Look at that." Beatrice must've noticed the change too. "Guess Louella finally decided to retire."

"Retire? I didn't know she wanted to retire."

"Yep. She wants to move to Boca. Uh-oh." For some reason, Beatrice's voice had grown soft. "You'd better turn into the parking lot, Missy."

I did as she asked and turned the steering wheel right. Once we made it safely into the lot, I pulled in front of the beauty salon and cut the engine. "Can I ask what we're doing here?"

"Look." She pointed at something just outside the passenger window, and I followed her gaze.

More butcher paper covered the lower half of the Kut N' Kurl's front door. On it, someone had printed COMING SOON in capital letters, followed by GOODE HAT-I-TUDE in fancy script.

"What in the world?" I said. "Please tell me that's not what I think it is."

Beatrice didn't bother to respond, since a drawing of a hat appeared over the very last letter of the new store's name. The crude drawing left no question as to what the shop would sell.

"Wow," she finally said. "Did you know about this?"

"Of course not. I didn't even know Louella was retiring. Remember?" I continued to stare at the sign, as if that might change its message. "I had no idea someone was going to open a hat shop around here."

I worried my lower lip as I contemplated the sign. The name sounded oddly familiar. Too familiar—especially with a hat sketched over the last *E*. "I have a bad feeling about this, Bea. I think I know who's behind it."

Chapter 11

Beatrice couldn't stop staring at the hand-drawn sign either. "You're kidding."

"I wish I was. I'll bet you anything it's that fashion blogger from New Orleans."

More than a year ago, Ambrose had taken me to Commander's Palace in New Orleans for our first date. Everything was wonderful until a stranger tried to hijack the night by approaching our table and asking Ambrose for an interview. The stranger's name was Antonella Goode, and she owned a website called Southern Comforts.

The blogger twice asked Ambrose to give her an interview on the spot, and twice he refused. At one point, Bo tried to divert her attention to me, since he wanted to give my new hat shop some much-needed publicity. He even suggested the stranger give me a call the following week and arrange to interview me, instead of him.

We both thought that was the end of that. But, miracle of miracles, the blogger called me the next Monday. She was vague at first, as if she was only calling to score points with Ambrose, but the more we chatted, the more animated she became.

We ended up doing the interview right then and there. Antonella's curiosity was insatiable. How'd I get my start? Where'd I learn to make hats? How did I get new clients? I thought she wanted background information for her story. And while I didn't give her any trade secrets, I probably said more than I should've, since I'd never been interviewed before and I reveled in the attention.

The interview appeared as a blog post the following Saturday on Southern Comforts, and it resulted in a half-dozen new clients and a follow-up story with a reporter from *Southern Living.*

"Why, that little she-devil," I said, more to myself than anyone else. "She only picked my brain because she wanted to open up her own hat store."

"So, you know the owner? Who is it?"

I turned to face Beatrice, my thoughts racing. "I think it's a woman named Antonella Goode. She's a fashion blogger, and she interviewed me for her website last August. Remember? It's called Southern Comforts. Guess I made my career sound too good to pass up."

"That's an understatement. But are you sure it's the same person?"

"Who else could it be? Look at the new store's name. It's not *that* common for a last name."

"I don't know." Beatrice didn't sound convinced. "But if it *is* her…what an underhanded thing to do. Are you going to call her?"

"I don't know yet." I brought my gaze back to the windshield. "But I think she ruined my appetite. There's no way I could enjoy a leisurely lunch at Miss Odilia's place now. Do you mind if we grab something to go and take it back to the store?"

"Of course not. I understand."

I pulled the car away from the bungalow and drove back to Highway 18. Thank goodness I'd traveled to Miss Odilia's place a million times before, since my brain switched to autopilot the moment we pulled onto the highway.

I couldn't even remember the last time I spoke with Antonella Goode. It must have happened right after the article appeared on Southern Comforts. I vaguely remembered thanking her for the story and telling her to stop by Crowning Glory so I could give her a hat.

Come to think of it…she never took me up on the offer. I'd given away several hats to fashion journalists over the last few years, including one to a reporter for *Today's Bride*, and they always appreciated the gesture. *Always.* But once I hung up the phone with Antonella, we never spoke again.

I pulled up to the entrance of Miss Odilia's Southern Eatery with memories still ping-ponging through my brain.

"Uh, Missy?"

The memories faded to black when I glanced at Beatrice. "I'm sorry. Did you say something?"

"I asked what you wanted to eat. I can run in and get it."

"That'd be great. I'll take the number two with a chicken breast and drumstick." Today was *not* the day for self-restraint. No amount of lettuce was going to provide the energy I needed to tackle my newest problem. "Pick out whatever you want too, and I'll pay for it."

I guided the car to a curb near the entrance, and then I shoved the gear in Park. I also pulled an Amex card from the pocket of my slacks. "Here. Take this. I'm going to sit out here and think while you get the food. Don't rush back to the car on my account. You can take your time inside with Miss Odilia."

"Will do." Beatrice hopped out of the car, taking the credit card with her. Once she slammed the passenger door shut, she bounded up the steps to the restaurant, where a paunchy, middle-aged man held open the front door for her.

What a strange morning. First, I had to suffer through another visit from Sabine d'Aulnay, and then I discovered a new hat shop planned to open down the road from mine. Worst of all was the niggling suspicion I might have helped Antonella by giving her so much information. *Darn me and my loose lips!*

I slowly retrieved the cell from my other pocket and dialed the number for Ambrose's Allure Couture. Maybe Bo could calm the panic that welled in my chest.

Luckily, he answered the call on the second ring. "Hi, Mitthy." His voice sounded garbled, as if he'd swallowed a mouthful of cotton.

"Hi, Bo. You won't believe what happened to me today."

"Wat's dat?"

"First of all, are you eating a sandwich? I can barely understand you."

He chuckled and dropped the receiver on something hard. A moment later, he came back on the line. "Sorry about that. Had to get some dress pins out of my mouth. Now, what's going on over there?"

I proceeded to tell him all about the demise of the Kut N' Kurl and the new hat shop that would take its place. I held my breath until I finished, and then I loudly exhaled. "So, that's what happened. She went behind my back, Ambrose."

"Okay. First of all, you don't even know it was her."

"*Pppffftt.*"

"Don't make that noise with me. I know it's a stretch, but what if there's another milliner named Goode?"

"I haven't heard of one. And don't you think that would be a huge coincidence? I do. There's really only one way to find out."

"What do you have in mind?"

"Could you please log on to your computer and search her website for me?" While I could just as easily access Southern Comforts on my cell,

I wanted to hear the news from Bo. Especially if it was bad. He could calm me down, and he might even be able to convince me none of this was my fault.

"Of course. Give me a sec."

Already, my panic level had begun to wane. I waited for him to return to the line a moment later.

"Okay," he said. "My computer's up and running. What's the name of the blog, again?"

"Southern Comforts."

"That's right. I remember the girl now. She tried to ambush me at Commander's Palace. Couldn't be more than five foot two, with a tiny face, like Tinkerbell."

"That's her." I quickly nodded, since we were finally getting somewhere. "But I didn't even tell you the worst part."

"Worst part? Now I'm curious."

"I think I may have helped her out."

"That's ridiculous. You're probably just being hard on yourself. The interview was more than a year ago. Don't you think she would've opened a store before now, if that was her plan?"

"Maybe she didn't have the funding. Or maybe she couldn't find the right property. There could be a million reasons why she waited so long."

"Calm down, Missy. We don't even know it's her at this point."

A few more seconds passed, and a few more clicks sounded in the background while Bo perused the Internet.

"Okay, I'm on her landing page," he finally said. "There are a lot of blog entries, going back about five years."

"Great. Could you please check the most recent ones and see if she mentions anything about opening a hat shop?"

Time stalled while Ambrose read the girl's blog in his studio. Just when I thought he might've gotten distracted by a stray link or two, he returned to the line.

"Uh-oh. You're not gonna like this, Missy."

That was all I needed to know. "Oh, shine." Just like that, the panic began to well again. "It's her, isn't it?"

"Yep. It's all here. She spent the last six months blogging about an old house she wanted to buy in Bleu Bayou. Said she took an online class in hat-making and she just needed to find a good property." A few more clicks sounded on the other end of the line. "She even talked about how there's another hat shop in Bleu Bayou, but it's really expensive."

"Expensive? Excuse me. How dare she—"

"Uh, Missy? Let's focus here. That's not the most important part. She can say anything she wants to say. But it looks like she's planning to open the store the third week of October."

My mind reeled. "But...but that's next week. How can she possibly get the shop up and running by then? She still has butcher paper over the windows, for heaven's sake."

"I don't know. But there's more. You're not gonna like this—"

"Stop saying that!" While none of this was Bo's fault, I had to take it out my frustration on someone, and he happened to be handy. "Whatever it is, I don't want to know. I can't handle any more bad news right now."

"But you have to hear this." He spoke gently, but firmly. "This really sucks, but nothing she's done is illegal. Underhanded, maybe, and sneaky as hell. But not illegal."

Darn him and his voice of reason. Of course, Bo was right. Anyone could hang out a shingle and call herself a milliner. That didn't mean she—or he—was any good at it or could make a hat or veil a bride would be proud to wear.

Unfortunately, first-time clients, and that included about 90 percent of all brides, often couldn't tell the difference between a quality hat and one with slipshod construction, until it was too late.

My job as a milliner was to show them what to look for: beautifully turned hems, soft as whispers but sturdy as steel; intricate patterns, layered and folded just so; and the artistic use of color that made even beige seem daring.

Like any milliner worth her salt, I'd spent years perfecting my skills. It took me a decade to master the different materials, play with shapes and forms, and work subtle fabric dyes into the mix. None of those things could be learned overnight.

"I feel sorry for her customers," I finally said. "They probably don't realize she's a phony. When they do, it'll be too late."

At that moment, something blurred on the other side of me, and I turned to see the door to the restaurant swing open. I expected to see Beatrice, but it was Zephirin Turcott, the new mayor of Bleu Bayou.

Today he wore a crisp navy suit with a paisley pocket square, and he squinted at the sun the moment he stepped on the landing. He was followed by a younger man, who carried a black leather portfolio under his arm.

"Hey, Ambrose?" I watched the two men regally descend the steps, one after the other. "I think I'd better hang up now. There's someone I want to talk to."

"Okay. I'll let you go. But don't do anything rash. We can talk about this when you get home tonight. Maybe we can figure something out."

"Gotcha. See you tonight. Love you."

"Luff youth too." Ambrose had apparently shoved a dress pin back in his mouth.

I hung up from the call and set the cell on the passenger seat. There had to be a way to stop Antonella Goode. And maybe—just maybe—it involved one of the two men who were headed my way.

Chapter 12

I hopped from the VW and scrambled onto the sidewalk in front of the restaurant. Luckily, most of the lunch crowd had moved inside, so I didn't have to worry about jumping into the path of an oncoming car.

"Excuse me," I called out. "Mayor Turcott?"

He stopped midstride. As I rushed to meet him, I extended my hand. Before he could return the gesture, though, his companion wedged in between us.

"Pardon me." The younger man obviously fancied himself the mayor's bodyguard. "Can I help you?"

"I, uh, have a quick question I'd like to ask the mayor. It'll just take a second."

"Sorry, but he's running late for a meeting. You'll have to call the office."

I peeked over the stranger's shoulder at the mayor, who looked puzzled.

"Is there a problem, Harrison?" the older man said.

"I really don't want to bother you, sir," I called out. "I'm your biggest fan." Which was true. I liked Zephirin Turcott's ideas about business a whole lot more than I liked his opponent's.

"Is that so?" The mayor's expression softened, once he realized I was more friend than foe. "Step aside, Harrison. Let the young lady through."

"Alright. If you say so." The self-appointed bodyguard reluctantly let me pass.

"That's better," the mayor said. "Now, what's your name, dear?"

"It's Melissa. Melissa DuBois." I extended my hand again. I wasn't offended by the endearment he used, although I could've been. After spending years in the deep South, I knew men and women of a certain age liked to use expressions like "dear," "honey," and "sweetheart" whenever they talked to someone younger. It happened all the time, and the speakers never meant any harm that I could tell.

He returned my handshake with a firm grasp. "It's nice to meet you, Miss DuBois. And thank you kindly for your support. It means a lot to know the community is on my side."

"Well, I certainly am. I especially like your plan to slash red tape at City Hall. My friends and I can't wait to see all the changes you're going to make."

"Now, I've got to warn you"—his hand fell away—"change won't happen overnight. We have to be patient."

At this point, the mayor's assistant seemed to realize he couldn't stop our conversation, because he backed away from us.

"That's true," I said. "Change doesn't happen overnight. But I do have a question for you."

"Fire away." When he smiled, the man's eyes twinkled like a friendly grandfather's.

"Well, I own a hat shop here in town for brides and their wedding parties." Better to start off slow and gradually build my case. It wouldn't do to accuse Antonella Goode of being underhanded right off the bat.

"I see. This town relies on business owners, like you. Good, hardworking Americans who provide much-needed services. You're the backbone of our community, you know."

I patiently waited for him to finish, since Mayor Turcott seemed to have mastered the art of the thirty-second sound bite. "Thank you, sir. My studio's in a building called the Factory, not too far from here."

"That *is* a coincidence. I ran my campaign from that building. Still have an office there, as a matter of fact. It's right next door to another wonderful American enterprise."

"Really? And what would that be?"

"A bakery." He playfully patted his midriff. "Quite a dangerous spot for my waistline."

"You must mean Pink Cake Boxes." We'd gotten sidetracked, but I didn't mind, since I wanted to get him on my good side. Maybe then he'd pay attention to what I had to say next. "Speaking of businesses...I'm a little concerned about a new one."

"Do tell."

"It's a new hat shop. It's going in right over there." I pointed in the general direction of Antonella's store. Although the restaurant blocked most of it, a sliver of lime-green stucco peeked around the far corner.

"I see." He followed my gaze. "What's wrong with it?"

"Well, there's some question as to whether the owner—her name is Antonella Goode—bothered to get the proper building permits."

It'd occurred to me when I spoke with Ambrose over the telephone. He'd mentioned Antonella planned to open her store Monday, which was only two days away. How in the world could she convert a beauty salon, with its very specific electrical requirements, into a hat store so quickly? Even if an electrician converted the wiring recently, that wouldn't give him or her enough time to have the work inspected. It normally took several weeks to get an inspector out to a property, given the backlog at the planning department. Antonella must've decided she'd rather take her chances with the city and hope no one found out.

I spoke from experience. When I first opened Crowning Glory two years ago, I followed the permit process to a T. Although I couldn't prove Antonella had done anything differently, I'd bet good money on it.

"Now, that's interesting." The mayor thought for a moment. "Goode, you say? Why, I think I know that family. If it's the same one, they're a fine family from up in New Orleans. Very involved in politics. Generous too."

My smile faltered. "You know them?" What were the odds the mayor knew Antonella Goode and her family? Slim to none, although apparently slim was enough in this case.

"Indeed. Why, they helped me get elected here. Some of my biggest supporters don't even live around here, you know."

"How interesting." It was time to backpedal if I wanted to save the conversation. "I'm sure she comes from a very fine family." Which was a lie, since I didn't know anything of the sort. "I just want to make sure all the business owners around here play by the same rules. You know, when it comes to getting building permits."

"How noble of you." By now, the mayor's smile had faded too. "But you just said one of the reasons you supported me was because of my stance on red tape. I'm trying to make it easier for the good people of Bleu Bayou to conduct business. Everything else will improve when that happens."

"I, uh, agree." My mind reeled as I struggled to refocus. I needed to change tack if I wanted to make my point without alienating the man standing in front of me. "But it's just as important for our shops to be safe for our customers. Don't you think so? That's why I appreciate all the things our city does to make sure a business is ready before it opens. You know, like checking the wiring, or, uh, the building's capacity." I limped to the end of my little speech, hoping it'd be enough.

"That's mighty noble of you, Miss DuBois. And I'll take it under advisement. By the way...do you volunteer in local politics?"

"Well, um." My smile shriveled even more. "Not really. I'd like to, but the shop keeps me pretty busy." Truth be told, my involvement in politics began and ended at the ballot box. It wasn't that I didn't care; I just didn't have enough time. "Someday I hope to get involved. Especially when my business slows down a little."

"That's what I thought." He *tsk*ed a few times. "There's never a perfect time, you know. Maybe you should try to get involved. Learn a little about what makes our city tick. Seems to me that's what the Goodes have done up in their little corner of the world."

It was as if the man's Teflon coat was melting before my eyes. Slowly, but surely, his true self had emerged. The merry twinkle in his eye? The glint of a seasoned politician. The *aw-shucks* persona? Cultivated through appearances at dozens of parades, town hall meetings, and front-lawn barbecues over the years. Make no mistake about it, Zephirin Turcott knew exactly what he was doing.

"You're...uh...correct, of course," I stammered. "Like I said, I'm hoping to get involved in local affairs when things slow down a little at my store."

"Mayor?" His assistant once more moved in between us. "We've got to get going. There's a follow-up to the press conference we had yesterday morning. The reporters want to hear more about the new health clinic. And if we don't hurry, you'll never make it onto their five o'clock newsfeeds."

"Guess my handler says it's time to go." He switched on the megawatt smile. "What a privilege to meet you, Miss DuBois. Best of luck with that little shop of yours."

"Thanks," I mumbled. "Nice to meet you too."

"If you have any more questions or concerns about my policies, please don't hesitate to contact my office."

"I'll do that." I never would, though. The look on his face when I mentioned Antonella Goode had told me everything I needed to know.

With that, the two men set off for a powder-blue convertible parked nearby. A very fancy convertible, as a matter of fact. Unless I was wrong, the car was a 1956 Thunderbird, with whitewall tires and a thick chrome bumper.

I turned away from the scene and walked back to my car. Only then did I notice Beatrice, who stood next to Ringo with a bulging paper sack from Odilia's restaurant.

"Who was that?" she asked, when I reached her.

"*That* was our illustrious mayor." I moved to the driver's side and carefully gripped the warmed door handle. Once I threw open the door and hopped inside, I waited for Beatrice to join me.

"You're kidding." She quickly slid onto the seat next to me. "You know the mayor?"

"I do now. But I think I made things worse for myself. What was I thinking?"

She shot me a funny look, but I didn't bother to explain. There'd be time enough to worry about the mayor once I had a chance to figure out my next move with Antonella. I could handle one problem at a time, and this latest one was a doozy.

Chapter 13

I clumsily fired up the engine, since my hands wouldn't cooperate, and slowly pulled away from the curb.

"C'mon," Beatrice urged. "Spill. What happened back there with the mayor?"

"I'll tell you what happened...I tried to talk to him about the new hat shop. Convince him to put the brakes on its grand opening. But everything backfired."

"Backfired? What do you mean?"

"I mean, he knows Antonella Goode's family." Even now, I couldn't believe my bad luck. "Ambrose confirmed she's the one who's behind the new hat shop. I called him when you were in the restaurant."

"Shut up!" Beatrice's eyes widened the moment she realized what she'd said. "Sorry about that, boss. I don't know why I keep saying it. Guess it's a bad habit."

"It's okay. I know you don't mean it." While I'd normally reprimand her, today I had too many other problems on my mind to worry about it. "Anyway, like I said, our conversation didn't go very well."

"I can't believe it. You're usually so good when you meet new people."

"Not today." I checked the flow of traffic over my left shoulder, and then I drove the car onto Highway 18. "I wanted to tell the mayor there's no way Antonella Goode could get the building permits in time for her new store to open. Ambrose said it's supposed to open Monday."

"This Monday? She's gonna be really busy this weekend."

"No doubt. And I don't think she'll have anything inspected before the store opens. She can't, not with such a tight timeline. Which means she's putting her customers—and her employees, if she hires any—at risk. Can you just imagine what'd happen if there was an electrical fire, or if she blocked the exits with packing boxes?"

"I don't know what to tell you, Missy." Beatrice seemed to want to say something good. "Will it make you feel better if I tell you Miss Odilia threw in some extra drumsticks?"

I gave her a slim smile. "Maybe. But I need to come up with a plan. Something that'll stop Antonella in her tracks."

We both fell silent during the short drive back to the Factory. While my conversation with the mayor didn't go well, at least it was short and we'd beaten everyone else back to work. Since I had my choice of parking spots, I pulled into one in the very first row.

By the time I hopped onto the warmed asphalt, Beatrice had outpaced me, and she swung the bag from Miss Odilia's casually back and forth as she walked.

"Wait up, Bea." I hurried to reach her, and together we headed for Crowning Glory. As soon as we arrived at the entrance, a blue-clad figure leaning against the wall straightened.

"Hey, Missy. I was just about to call you."

"Hi, Lance." I jimmied a key into the shop's front door. "Let's get you inside."

I quickly headed into the studio ahead of the detective. It wasn't the bright sunshine that made me hurry indoors, but my need for privacy. I didn't want my neighbors to know I sometimes teamed up with Bleu Bayou's finest to help solve murder cases. It wouldn't do for them to think their resident milliner dabbled in something as grisly as that.

"The ME gave me some more info." Lance spoke over his shoulder as he strode to the counter. "Looks like the killer gave Ruby alcohol in addition to the knockout drug."

"First thing in the morning?" I moved over to where he stood, and then I stashed my keys in a drawer under the counter. "How'd they pull that off?"

"Good question. But it's a common trick. Alcohol makes a drug like that twice as potent."

Beatrice lingered by the front entrance, since she rightly suspected we wouldn't be able to include her in our conversation. "I think I'll leave you two alone," she finally said, as she turned toward the workroom. "See you later, Lance."

I waited until she moved out of earshot. "So, it sounds like the killer did some research first."

"Apparently so. He gave her just enough alcohol to make the drug more potent, but not so much that Ruby would question it."

I threw him a sideways glance. "Or *she* did that. We can't keep assuming the killer is a male."

"You're right." He chuckled softly. "I always knew you should've been a detective. We would've made a great team. Kinda like Mulder and Scully."

"Yeah, right." While I appreciated the *X-Files* reference, I wasn't about to go chasing after the supernatural with Lance. "Anyway, that *is* interesting. How'd the ME find out about the alcohol?"

"He analyzed the blood in her veins. It's the best way to determine whether someone dosed the victim with alcohol."

Before Lance could say more, the door to the studio swung open. In stepped Hollis, whose gaze flitted around the room.

"We're over here, Hollis," I called out.

He acknowledged me with a nod. Instead of hurrying toward us, though, he slowly threaded his way through the displays stiff-armed, as if he was afraid to touch anything. He seemed worried about the shiny sequins, fluffy tulle, and delicate feathers all around him.

"It's okay," I said. "You won't break anything."

He didn't relax, despite my reassurances. When he finally reached the counter, he plopped onto a bar stool. "Whew. I made it."

"Hi, Hollis," Lance said. "What's up with you?"

The boy didn't answer right away, and something about his demeanor bothered me.

"Is everything okay, Hollis?" I asked.

"No. Not really."

He wouldn't look at me either. "C'mon now. Something's happened."

"Okay, fine." He pulled a cell from the pocket of his Nike shorts and tossed it on the counter. "It's this."

"You broke your phone?" Everything about the phone looked fine to me, except for a leering skeleton on the case, of course. "You can borrow my phone anytime you want."

"That's not it, Miss DuBois."

"Then what's going on?" Lance asked. "Are you in trouble?"

"Here's the thing," he said. "I don't know what's going on. I got the weirdest phone call this morning, and it kinda freaked me out."

Lance and I exchanged quick looks. While I desperately wanted to ask a follow-up question, Lance was the pro when it came to interrogating people. He needed to lead the conversation and not me.

"Did you know the caller?" Sure enough, Lance automatically switched into cop mode.

"I don't think so," Hollis said. "But it was hard to tell. It sounded like a guy's voice, but it was all echo-y. I could barely understand him."

Uh-oh. Someone had called Hollis using a voice scrambler, which was never a good sign. I bit my tongue and let the conversation continue without me.

"What did the caller say?" Lance asked.

"He wanted me to stay away from Grandma's property. At least, that's what I think he said."

"Did he threaten you?" Lance asked.

"Not exactly. But he told me to stay away from the river house. Or else."

"Or else, what?"

"He said I'd be sorry." Hollis finally turned to me for a reaction, which I couldn't ignore.

"You poor thing," I said. "That had to be terrifying."

"It creeped me out," he said. "What if the guy means it?"

Once more, his gaze sought mine. While Lance was the expert, Hollis and I shared a past, and I couldn't help but support him. "He could be bluffing, you know. Maybe it was a crank phone call."

"But he sounded serious," Hollis said.

"How did you know it was a guy who called you?" While we had other things to worry about, Hollis kept repeating something that bothered me. "It could've been a girl. It's hard to tell with a voice scrambler."

"Oh yeah. You're right," he said. "I guess I don't know, now that you mention it. I was too freaked out by the echo."

"Okay, let's get back to the basics," Lance said. "First of all, it's easy enough to tell where a call comes from." He reached over and grabbed Hollis's cell phone. Once he tapped the screen, he laid it down again. "Figures. The person used an app to block the telephone number."

It was a move I'd seen before. Early last year, a local wedding planner died in the parking lot behind my studio, and her murderer sent me a text message. But the killer was smart enough to block the cell number from appearing on my screen so I couldn't figure out who'd called.

"Gosh, Lance. This is just like what happened last year. Remember that?"

"Do I," he said. "These phone apps keep getting better and better. Which makes my job even harder. Say, Hollis. Do you mind if I keep your cell for a while? I want to put a tracer on it."

The teen immediately frowned. "For how long?"

"Just a few hours. We've got a 'stingray' device back at headquarters that one of the tech guys can install."

Now *there* was a term I'd never heard before. While I knew all about voice scramblers and call blockers, I'd never come across something called a stingray. "What are you talking about?"

"It's a cell phone interceptor," he answered. "It mimics the signals of a cell tower, so your caller's cell will try to connect to it if he—or she—calls you again. That way I can get the location, and we'll know who we're dealing with."

"That's way cool." Hollis sounded impressed...so impressed he momentarily forgot he was about to lose his cell phone. "It sounds like something from a sci-fi movie."

"Even better than that," Lance said. "The military developed it to fight terrorists."

As impressive as that was, one problem remained. "But what if the person doesn't call back?" I asked.

"Oh, they will." Lance glanced at Hollis again. "Did you hang up on them, or was it the other way around?"

"I think I hung up first," Hollis said. "I couldn't stand hearing that voice."

"Then they'll definitely try to call you again. And I've got an idea."

Lance angled his shoulders away from me, as if he knew I wasn't going to like what he was about to say. Ever since we were little kids, I could read his body language like an open book.

"Uh-oh," I said. "What's on your mind?"

"Hollis needs to go back to the river house." He wouldn't look at me while he spoke. "We'll trace the call from there."

"But—"

"Hold on, Missy. Let me finish."

I fell silent, which wasn't easy, given every instinct urged me to protect Hollis. It had started back on the bayou, when I saw the look on his face after he'd found his grandmother's clog. The feeling only intensified when he fell asleep on my shoulder in the cruiser on the way back from the police station. And now this.

"You know, you don't have to go back home," I quickly told the teen.

Lance frowned at me, clearly annoyed. "Do you mind? We need to find out who called him. If we can trace the call, we can probably catch the killer."

"But why does he have to go home for that?"

"Because the stingray works best if two phones are close together. When the killer realizes Hollis has gone back home, the person is bound to make another call from the property. Then we can trace it and see who the phone's registered to."

"But it's not safe, Lance."

"Look...I'll even request a backup unit for the woods. And I'll stay with Hollis, so he's never alone."

"Uh, guys?" Hollis said. "I'm right here. You don't have to talk over my head. I get it."

We both ignored him. "I still don't like it, Lance." Much as I admired the newfangled police technology, I couldn't imagine using Hollis as a guinea pig. "There's no way Hollis should go back to the river house when Ruby's killer is running loose."

"This isn't your decision, Missy. And he'll be safer with me than with anyone else."

Darn him and his firepower. Of course he was right. While Lance carried a Glock 22, the most sinister thing I owned was a pair of pinking shears. Neither I, nor Ambrose, had quick access to a loaded handgun or a backup unit. "I dunno—"

"It's okay," Hollis interrupted. "I don't mind, Miss DuBois. You've been so nice to me. But I kinda want to go home anyway. I didn't much sleep last night, and I'm bushed. No offense, but your fiancé snores."

"Be that as it may"—my resolve weakened in the face of so much opposition—"I don't want to let you out of my sight."

"Really, it's okay," Hollis said. "I trust Detective LaPorte."

"Thanks." Lance reached for his phone, which he kept in his front pocket. "I'll request the surveillance unit right now. Once I drop off your phone at headquarters, I'll head over to your grandma's house."

"Gotcha." Unlike me, Hollis didn't seem worried by this latest turn of events. "I'll go over to Miss DuBois's place and pack up my stuff."

"By the way," I asked, "did you drive over here?" Outside of his grandmother's Jeep, Hollis didn't have access to a car, as far as I knew.

"Your neighbor drove me over," he said. "He's been waiting for me in the parking lot all this time."

Of course. "You must mean Mr. Dupre." Leave it to Hank to help Hollis navigate his way to my studio when the boy needed help. "Please tell him I said thank you."

"No problem. See ya later."

"I've gotta head out too," Lance said. "Try not to worry, okay?"

With that, they both retreated from the shop. Hollis seemed much more relaxed than when he'd first arrived, since his arms swung freely now, and Lance maintained the straight-backed gait I'd come to recognize.

The room fell silent for a moment or two, until Beatrice stuck her head around the door to the workroom and peered around the studio.

"Everyone gone?" Her gaze swept the shop from front to back.

"Yeah, they're gone. You can come out now."

She made her way to the counter with a Chinet paper plate balanced on her palm. On it she'd piled some fried chicken and rolls, and a streak of something bronze and runny marred her chin. "I'm sorry, but I couldn't wait. I started lunch without you."

Aha. Barbecue sauce. "That's okay. I'm really not that hungry anyway."

To be honest, I'd forgotten all about lunch. Once Lance told me his plan for Hollis, everything else flew out the window. How could Lance know for sure that nothing bad would happen to Hollis if he returned to the river? After everything the boy had been through, I wanted him to feel safe for once.

"Are you okay?" Beatrice's voice brought me back to the present.

"Huh? What?"

"I asked if you're okay. You look worried."

"I am. I think I just agreed to something I shouldn't have. Something I'm going to regret before this is all over."

Chapter 14

I put aside my misgivings about Hollis long enough to take a few bites of the drumstick Beatrice offered me. We sat at the counter, where I nibbled the chicken and she polished off a bottle of Aquafina.

"You haven't even tried a biscuit yet." She pushed one of hers toward me in a vain attempt to get me to eat. "We can't let all this good food go to waste."

"I'm just not that hungry." I tossed the half-eaten chicken on my plate, next to the roll. "Remember what you said about today being weird? You don't know the half of it. Hollis just told us he got a crank phone call from someone who threatened him. The caller told him not to go back to Ruby's house…or else."

"Or else what?"

"That's a great question. Lance can't even trace the call because the person used an app to block it. This isn't a small-time crook we're talking about here. The person who killed Ruby really knew what they were doing."

"That's creepy." Beatrice wiped her lips with a napkin before she rose. "Well, you're not gonna eat lunch, and I'm as stuffed as a tick. I might as well go back to work."

"Yeah, me too."

She paused to study me. "I don't think that's a good idea. You look kinda pale, to be honest."

"Thanks. That makes me feel a whole lot better."

"I'm serious. You can't keep going on like this. Maybe you should take some time off this afternoon. Get some rest, or at least some fresh air."

I waved away her concern. "Sorry, but I don't think that's gonna happen. I have too many things to do. Thanks for worrying about me, though."

"You know you could just as easily work out of your house, don't you? You'd probably get a lot more done too." She was like a dog with a chew toy once she got a notion.

"But everything I need is here."

"Then I'll help you pack up some supplies. There's no reason for you to stay. Plus, you know how quiet it gets here Friday afternoons."

I contemplated her offer. "That's true. It's like a ghost town this close to the weekend. Maybe you're right."

"I know I am. I'll watch the store, and I promise to call if anything comes up. Scout's honor." She held up two fingers in a Boy Scout salute.

"Okay, then. Maybe I'll take a long walk too. It's such a nice day outside, and my muscles are wound tighter than a two-dollar watch." It was something my grandpa used to say, but I could tell it meant nothing to Beatrice, because she didn't respond. "My grandpa used to tell me that all the time. It means someone's muscles are too stiff."

"Whatever. You can haul out whatever old-timey saying you want, as long as you take some time off."

"Alright. You convinced me." I rose from the counter and grabbed a folder labeled ACCOUNTS RECEIVABLE from under the cash register, where I also found my car keys. "Guess there's no use in me staying here and driving myself crazy. Maybe a change of scenery will do me good."

"Atta girl. I'll call you if anything happens."

My mind made up, I headed for the front door. "Thanks, Beatrice!" I traipsed across the welcome mat.

A gentle breeze brushed my face the moment I stepped outside. A few cars passed me on their way to the exit, but traffic had noticeably thinned since this morning. By four on a Friday, not a single car would remain in the lot. Except for Beatrice's pink Ford pickup, of course.

It used to bother me whenever the other shopkeepers skipped out of work early while I stayed behind to mind the store, like Beatrice was doing for me now.

Ever since I opened Crowning Glory, I'd walked past one locked shop after another whenever I closed the studio late at night. Most days, I worked until six, seven, or eight—Fridays included—while everyone else bolted out of the Factory.

Maybe that was why the thought of Antonella opening another hat store in town bothered me so much. I liked to think I'd earned my success the old-fashioned way, with a lot of sweat, a few hundred tears, and oodles of sleepless nights.

To think someone could watch a few videos on YouTube and proclaim herself a milliner was an insult not only to me, but to everyone in my industry.

Lost in thought, I started down the sidewalk, but before I got very far, someone rushed past me. "Whoa!"

The offender immediately stopped. "Didn't see ya there. Sorry 'bout dat." It was an old man in a chartreuse camp shirt that covered his lanky frame like a construction worker's caution vest. He stood at least six five, and a dark suntan colored his scalp and cheeks.

"Mr. Gaudet?"

The swamp boat captain didn't seem to remember me, though, because he stared straight ahead.

"It's me...Melissa DuBois. We met the other day on Ruby Oubre's dock."

He finally looked at me after he'd fiddled with something behind his left ear. "Wat's dat ya say?"

"It's Melissa DuBois. M-I-S-S-Y."

"Gah-lee. Ya don't have ta shout, for goodness' sakes. I can hear ya jus' fine now."

Chastised, I lowered my voice again. "I'm a little surprised to see you here." The captain didn't strike me as the type who'd shop at the bridal stores in the Factory.

"Gots ta drop off sumptin' inside. What'cha doin' here?"

"I work here. I own a hat studio called Crowning Glory." I motioned over my shoulder to the shop. When I finished, my gaze traveled to something he held by his side. It was a plastic bag, and he'd scrawled Suite 221 on a Post-it Note taped to the front. "I see you know our mayor."

"Pardon?" he asked.

"Your package. You must know the mayor."

He drew his hand away from me. "Not really."

"I thought you must know him by the address on your package. I only met him this morning."

While all this chitchat was good and well, the clear sky and gentle breeze called out to me. "Well, I should get going. I'll see you around."

Before I could move, though, the captain reached out for my arm. "One more ting." His gaze bore into mine. "You tell dat Hollis he needs to watch hisself. Shouldn't be talkin' to his elders like dat."

I started, surprised by the tone of his voice. "Maybe so, but we all have to remember he's had a horrible week. He lost his grandmother, for goodness' sakes."

"But dat's not ma fault. No need for him to cuss me out on a-count a dat."

"I seem to recall you had some choice words for him too. He's a teenager."
I couldn't imagine why the captain couldn't let bygones be bygones in light
of everything that had happened.

"Dat's not da first time we done tussled. Don' let dat boy fool you. He
ain't no saint. He knows it, an' I know it."

We'd obviously reached a stalemate. If I didn't leave now, Ambrose
would have to dash out of his studio and referee another fight. "Look, I
don't know what's going on between you two, but it's really none of my
business. Just give Hollis some space. He's suffered a big loss."

"Here's da thing." Finally, the captain released my arm. "I went over
ta Ruby's place to help dat boy out. Ain't no way he can take care 'a dat
property by hisself. He's gonna need to sell it sometime. Might as well
face facts and get on wit' it."

"But Ruby only died a day ago. There's no need to rush Hollis into
making a decision about *anything* right now."

"Dat's what you tink. Folks be talkin' 'bout me back in town now. Dey
know I sent Ruby dat letter."

"Letter?" I quickly rifled through my memory bank but came up empty.
"What letter?"

"Jus' a little sumptin' Mr. Dupre done wrote up for me."

At the mention of Hank, the door to my memory vault flew wide open.
Of course. The letter of intent I'd spied on Ruby's coffee table, back there
in her mobile home. Hank had mentioned it to me the other day.

"That's right. You're the one who offered to buy her land."

"Shoulda mailed out dat letter a long time ago. Woulda stopped folks
from talkin' 'bout me now. It jus' don' look good."

Neither does fighting with her grandson, I wanted to remind him. But
I refrained, since the captain didn't seem interested in my opinion.

Sure enough, he turned to leave before I could respond. I watched him
limp away, his bright green camp shirt growing smaller and smaller, until
it finally disappeared when he ducked into the glass atrium that divided
the Factory in two.

It took me two laps around the Factory's parking lot to put the episode
behind me. Once I'd finally cleared my head, I decided to drive downtown
and visit Homestyle Hardware, which was a local do-it-yourself shop and
garden store.

While I didn't find any new household decorations during my shopping
trip, like I'd hoped, I did spy an adorable bubblegum-pink birdhouse that
matched the paint on the outside of my rent house. Maybe Ambrose would
help me hang it on one of the pin oaks in our backyard when he got home.

After shopping a bit more, I drove back to the cottage with my treasure tucked beside me on the passenger seat, ready to show it off. My excitement waned the minute I pulled into the driveway, though, because Ambrose's Audi was nowhere to be found. He was supposed to work from home this afternoon, to make up for all the extra hours he'd been logging at Ambrose's Allure Couture. Something must have happened to change that plan.

I parked Ringo on the empty driveway and glumly headed inside. Silence enveloped me as I trekked through the empty house and stepped into the kitchen.

I immediately spied a piece of paper on top of the Black and Decker toaster. It was a note, with two sentences in that slanted handwriting of Ambrose's. "Back at work until who knows when. Don't wait up."

Oh, sugar. I shouldn't have been surprised, though. Although the stream of wedding clients had trickled to a drizzle for most of us at the Factory, the same couldn't be said for Ambrose. Once the brides went away, he took calls from fashion catalogs, which worked six months in advance and always asked him to create candy-colored ballgowns for their spring covers.

Too bad he wouldn't be home until late. I had a thousand and one things to discuss with him, including my conversation with the mayor, Lance's latest plan for Hollis, and the strange run-in with Captain Gaudet.

It seemed our conversation would have to wait for now. While my spirit was willing, my body had a mind of its own, and I headed for the bedroom, where I flopped onto the mattress facedown.

Chapter 15

I awoke the next morning to the squeal of a kiskadee outside my bedroom window. The bird sounded exactly like a squeaky toy Hank Dupre sometimes threw to his schnauzer in their yard next door. *Squee. Squee. Squee.*

My head lolled against the pillow as the noise urged me awake. I couldn't help but think about everything that'd happened over the past few days as I slowly came to. The memories brought up so many questions I couldn't answer, but ones I also couldn't forget.

What *did* happen to Ruby, out there on the bayou? A strong, confident woman, she grew up swimming in the Atchafalaya River, for heaven's sake, and she knew those waters better than anyone else. How could she have drowned only yards from her home?

And what about Hollis's mystery caller? Why would anyone care whether Hollis returned to his grandmother's land or not? It didn't change anything, as far as I knew, and it wouldn't benefit anyone else if he stayed away. Or would it?

And finally...what should I do about my newfound competition? Although Antonella Goode wasn't a real milliner, her clients wouldn't know that. She'd leave behind a trail of broken hearts, and, in my experience, nothing was worse than a distraught bride.

The questions needled me until I finally rolled off the mattress and trudged down the hall. When I reached the kitchen, I leaned against the doorjamb to let my eyes adjust to the brightness.

Unlike my dim bedroom down the hall, here every light blazed, including the expensive incandescent bulbs screwed into the pendant lights over the kitchen counter.

Ambrose normally double-checked the lights at night to make sure they were off before he went to bed. Only one thing could explain the oversight. My fiancé must've been dead to the world by the time he finally got home from work.

Maybe I should spoil him a little this morning. I'd been so preoccupied with my own problems lately, I'd completely forgotten about his. He was the one who stayed up late last night to work on the spring ball gowns, the one who let me bring Hollis into our house with no questions asked, and the one who always took my calls at work—no matter how urgent or how silly—without a second thought. Maybe I should do something nice for him for a change.

For starters, he'd probably wake up hungry this morning, and our pantry was about as bare as Old Mother Hubbard's cupboard. Odds were good he couldn't rustle a single bagel, an overdue egg, or a spongy granola bar if he tried.

The solution, of course, was for me to visit a certain donut store down the road. Dippin' Donuts offered the best beignets in southern Louisiana, not to mention gourmet coffee to die for. But that would mean interacting with the bakery's owner, Grady Sebastian.

But maybe I could swallow my pride—just this once—and snag some beignets and gourmet coffee for Ambrose.

My mind made up, I backtracked to the bedroom, where I quickly threw on a tattered Vanderbilt T-shirt and my Lululemon sweats. Then I tiptoed through the quiet house and made my way to the driveway.

Once I pulled onto the highway, I settled in for the short drive. Traffic was blessedly light, given the early hour, and soon the flaming neon arrow that shot from the roof of Dippin' Donuts appeared on the horizon like a bright red checkmark.

I approached the parking lot, where I took a hard left and scanned the available spots. Unlike the roadway next to it, the parking lot had filled with sturdy pickups, dusty minivans, and a motorcycle or two. After circling the lot once, I snagged a sliver of asphalt between a Chevy Silverado and an equally large Ford F-150. From there it was only a hop, skip, and a jump to the front door, which Grady had propped open with an old Community Coffee can filled with pea gravel.

One foot inside the entrance and the heavenly aroma of choux paste, melted butter, and confectioners' sugar washed over me. It pulled me into the shop and gave me an invisible nudge toward a line of customers. The line stretched from the front door to a trio of display cases filled with strawberry scones, blueberry coffee cakes, cherry hand pies, and more beignets than you could shake a stick at.

Grady manned the counter with one of his employees, only he didn't notice me until it was my turn to place an order.

"I'd like a half-dozen beignets, please, and two large coffees."

His head jerked up with a start. "Missy? I haven' seen you in a dog's age."

I returned his gaze, which was a huge mistake. I'd forgotten about his gorgeous blue eyes, the color of a freshwater lake, the dimple that cleft his chin in two, and the whimsical tattoo of a chef's whisk on his muscled biceps.

I allowed myself one last ogle before I cleared my throat. "I've been really busy lately. Guess I haven't had time to do much of anything."

"Well, I've missed seeing you around here. How've you been?"

The comment startled me. This was the guy who talked nonstop about himself during our one and only date, the man who never once asked about my life.

The evening had started out promisingly enough. He'd taken me to a lively restaurant and dance hall on the outskirts of town called Antoine's Country Kitchen. The place offered everything for a night of fun—delicious crawfish étouffée, cold ale from Chappapeela Farms Brewery, and a real zydeco band, complete with rubboard and bass guitar.

Only one thing soured the evening, Grady's monologue. He dissected every major football game he'd ever quarterbacked for the Bleu Bayou Fighting Tigers. He remembered them all, including a heartbreaking loss at the state championship his senior year, when he threw a magnificent spiral pass that his wide receiver somehow fumbled.

Although ten years had come and gone since then, Grady still mourned the loss. To top it off, he ordered dinner for me afterward without even asking what I wanted. Was it any wonder I ignored his phone calls for weeks until he finally gave up?

But now, he suddenly wanted to know how I'd been.

"I guess I've been good. Until Thursday, that is."

"Yeah, I heard about Ruby's death. How's Hollis holding up?"

"As well as can be expected. I wish people would stop badgering him. Asking him when he's going to sell his grandmother's property and move off the river. They act like he has to make a decision *this very minute* or they'll explode with curiosity."

He chuckled sadly. "You have to understand why people care so much. There wasn't much land left for the regular folks once the lumber company moved in. Now it's like a national treasure. People would sell their souls to get a little slice of that heaven."

"So I've heard. But it's not just about the land. Ruby raised Hollis. It's like he lost his mom, but no one seems to realize that."

"Give them time. Let the drama die down first."

"You know there's some question about how she died, right?" I glanced over my shoulder. "It's an open investigation, so I can't really talk about it, but the medical examiner is looking at homicide."

"Lord knows I have some opinions about what could've happened. Why don't I call you later, so we can discuss it in private?"

My jaw tensed. For all I knew, Grady was using the situation with Ruby to get closer to me. Just in case, I brought out my favorite maneuver for averting unwanted questions, misdirection. "Say…look at this place! I've never seen so many people in here. Is the rush a new thing?"

"Pretty much." He seemed momentarily distracted. "It came after they finally opened the new off-ramp to the freeway. Not that I'm complaining, mind you."

Thank goodness he didn't seem to mind when I steered the conversation onto safe ground again. "And can I have those beignets to go, please? I really shouldn't hold up the line anymore."

"That's okay. There are two of us working the counter today." He slowly lifted a wax-paper sack from a stack in front of him. "I've got a great idea. I'm about to go on break. Why don't I keep you company while you eat? We can catch up."

"They're not all for me. I want to bring some back home to my fiancé. His name is Ambrose. Remember?"

Grady winced as he pulled the first beignet from the case and dropped it in the sack. "Yeah, that's right. You're engaged. I forgot about that."

"Maybe some other time. I want to drop off the beignets at the house before I run some errands. Poor Ambrose got home really late last night."

Grady seemed distracted as he filled the sack. "Okay. But I may have some news for you too. About a certain store that's going to open up."

"Are you talking about the new hat shop?" Not that I wanted to steal his thunder, but it sounded like he was trying to stall me by mentioning Antonella's shop. "I drove by it yesterday with Beatrice."

"So you already know about it, huh? I met the owner yesterday."

"Did you know she's not even a trained hatmaker?" I couldn't keep the irritation from my voice. "Turns out she's a fashion blogger from New Orleans. She's just trying to make a quick buck off the brides who come here to get married. It's really bothering me, to tell you the truth."

"I can tell," he said. "She made it sound like she's been making hats for years. Apparently, she's got everyone fooled."

"Why do you say that?"

"She told me the city's throwing a huge blowout for her grand opening." He shrugged as he passed the full sack across the counter.

"A blowout?" While I knew some things about Good Hat-i-tudes, apparently I didn't know everything. "I didn't hear anything about it."

"The people down at the business development office promised her a big celebration. Marching band, barbecue dinner, the works. The mayor's even gonna speak."

"I had no idea." The news took a moment to register. Apparently, I'd been so busy between Ruby's death and Hollis's living arrangements, not to mention my own hat shop, I'd completely missed the announcement. "Why didn't she advertise it?"

"The flyers are going up this weekend. That's why Antonella...I mean, Toni...came in here. She asked me to put some flyers in the bakery's window."

"She did, huh? Toni. You don't say..."

He must've noticed my dismay. "I didn't ask for them. She just gave them to me. But I won't put them up if you don't want me to."

Sure enough, I glanced over his shoulder and spied a stack of colorful flyers next to the Bunn coffee machine. The top one showed a cartoon wedding veil complete with scalloped edges and a curlicued headpiece.

"Would you mind leaving them there for a little bit?" I asked. "I want to check out that hat store first. See what's really going on."

"Sure. No problem. It's no skin off my nose."

"Thanks. Thanks a lot."

"To be honest, I think she just wanted to flirt with me. She kept asking about my football picture over there." He jerked his chin toward a faded eight-by-ten photo he'd thumbtacked to the wall. The picture showed twelve teenage boys in steel-gray jerseys with scrawny arms and fuzzy chins.

"Geesh," he said. "Guess some people can't get over their high-school days."

Given a better mood, I might've rolled my eyes, but I didn't have it in me at the moment. Instead, I took the bag and turned to leave. "That's something, all right. Thanks again for holding off on the flyers. I'll let you know what I find out."

"Hey...I almost forgot your coffees." He motioned for me to wait while he grabbed two Styrofoam cups from a stack near the Bunn machine.

"You could always talk to the people over at City Hall." He spoke over his shoulder as he placed the cups under the nozzles. "Let 'em know what's up."

"I was hoping I'd have a stronger case before I did that. So far, the only thing she's done wrong is to convert a beauty shop into a hat store without getting any permits."

"Well, that's enough." He turned around again and placed the full cups in a cardboard carryall, which he slid across the counter. "I'll keep my ears open for you too. I'll let you know if I hear anything else. And by the way...this is on the house."

"Thanks, Grady." *Maybe I judged him a bit too harshly. Nah.* "Guess I might see you there on Monday."

"You're going to the grand opening?" he asked. "I thought you didn't like her."

"Oh, I don't like her. She used me to get information to open her store. But I can't pass up the chance to look around a little." I tucked the sack of beignets next to the coffees and backed away from the display case. "See you Monday."

"You too." He reluctantly shifted his attention to the next customer in line.

The coffee sloshed a bit as I made my way out of the bakery, so I took my time settling the carryall into the passenger seat of the Volkswagen. Then I slid behind the steering wheel and fired up the ignition.

Grady's words kept echoing through my mind, though. A big blowout. Marching band...barbecue...the works. What was *that* all about?

The day I opened Crowning Glory, I'd stood by the front door with a cheesy smile on my face and a heavy tray of homemade cookies in my hands. I'd spent hours the night before rolling the dough into miniature hats, which I garnished with whisper-thin fondant headbands and sugar flowers made with gum paste.

Some people looked askance when I offered them a cookie, since we both knew they'd never step foot in my store. But I didn't care. I offered the treats to everyone, including a FedEx driver, some Catholic schoolkids who delivered flowers for extra cash, and even a plumber who came to repair my leaky faucet.

To know the city had offered Antonella Goode a full-blown celebration boggled my mind. Not that I wanted to be petty, but where was *my* marching band, or barbecued brisket, or welcome speech from the mayor? Where was the city when Ambrose opened his wedding gown studio, or Bettina launched Pink Cake Boxes? Dozens of small business people around here had poured their hearts and souls into new businesses, yet no one from City Hall seemed to give a lick. It didn't seem right, or fair.

I steadied a coffee cup with my free hand as I drove out of the parking lot and turned left onto the highway. One sugarcane field after another passed by my window, but I barely noticed them. Finally, I arrived at a stop sign, which startled me awake. I'd somehow turned the wrong way on Highway 18 and was heading away from my cottage, instead of toward it.

Unless I made an immediate U-turn, I'd arrive at the sherbet-colored bungalow that housed Goode Hat-i-tudes in only a few minutes.

My subconscious must've known all along that was where I wanted to go, because I didn't make the U-turn.

Chapter 16

The rest of the drive whizzed by, once I accepted the new plan. Odds were good Ambrose was still asleep anyway, and I could always warm his coffee in the microwave when I returned to the cottage.

After driving a few more minutes, I spied the trio of bungalows, with their pastel paint, pitched roofs, and concrete stoops. They reminded me of the candy-colored houses on San Francisco's Postcard Row, those "painted ladies" tourists loved to photograph with their cell phones.

I turned the steering wheel right and pulled into the parking lot behind a white work van emblazoned with a logo for Al's Heating & Air-Conditioning. The logo showed a smiling snowman with a giant pair of sunglasses perched on the end of a carrot nose.

I followed the snowman onto the lot and parked next to the work van. I couldn't wait to see what was behind the plate-glass window covered in butcher paper at Goode Hat-i-tudes.

Oh, shine! It wasn't open. Only a sliver of window showed above the butcher paper, and the room behind it was dark and still. *Now what?* Before I could fret too much, a pudgy man in navy coveralls emerged from the van next to me with a toolbox in his hand and an enormous set of keys. He stopped in front of the hat store, where he inserted one of the keys into the lock, and miraculously, the door swung open.

"Yoo-hoo." I quickly scrambled from the VW and followed him onto the sidewalk. "Hello?"

He didn't turn, which meant he probably couldn't hear me, but he seemed to notice me when he spied my reflection in the window.

Then he couldn't spin around fast enough. "Why, hello there."

I tried to ignore his flirty tone. "Hello. Are you working at the new hat shop today?"

"As a matter of fact, I am. Are you the owner?"

"No. Not exactly. But I know her. She's...um...a friend of mine." Hopefully, God would forgive me for the fib, even if Antonella might not.

"I see." He scanned me from head to toe, and he seemed to like what he saw, because he smiled again. "She's a lucky friend."

"Uh, yeah. Do you think you could let me inside her store? I promised to pick something up for her, but she forgot to give me a key." By now, I'd dug a hole so deep with my lies, it wouldn't matter if I layered on another fib or two. Would it?

"You're a friend of hers, huh? Well, okay. I never could say no to a pretty lady. My name's Dan." He thrust out his hand, which was streaked with compressor fluid. Since I worked around pale fabrics so much, I'd developed an aversion to oily lubricants, but this time it was worth the risk, and I put my hand in his.

"Nice to meet you." I carefully shook his hand. "I'm so glad you came along when you did."

"You and me both. C'mon. Follow me."

He motioned for me to follow him into the dark shop. I hesitated until I remembered it was Saturday morning, after all, and plenty of folks would be trucking cargo to and from the storage units next door or eating breakfast at Odilia's restaurant nearby. I could always holler for help if I needed it.

Just as I stepped over the threshold, the overheads clicked on and yellow light washed across the room.

I was surrounded by a bunch of antique tables, some draped in old bedsheets, and others bare. Large ones, small ones, and all of them decorated with turned legs and ball-and-claw feet. The tables looked suspiciously like the antiques I'd placed in my own hat shop, but that was probably just a coincidence.

"What did you say your name was again?" The repairman had moved to a wall to check on a thermostat that hung there.

"I didn't say. But it's Melissa DuBois. I own a hat studio at the place they call the Factory."

"A hat studio, huh? Just like your friend. Come to think of it...I did some work over at the Factory once. Replaced a grill cover for a fellow that makes wedding dresses. Do you know him?"

I nodded, my eyes still adjusting to the brash overheads. "Yes, that's my fiancé. My shop is next door to his."

"You don't say." The mention of a fiancé seemed to take the wind out of Dan's sails, and he quickly returned his attention to the temperature gauge. "Anyway, your friend called me out of the blue yesterday. Caught me by surprise. I didn't think she'd want me to come back here."

"Really? Why not?"

He shrugged. "She didn't like what I had to say last time."

Interesting. Sometimes, the key to getting more information from someone was to repeat the very last thing he'd said. Especially when you had no idea what he was talking about. "She didn't like it, huh?"

"Nope. Not one bit." He fiddled with the gauge as he spoke. "I checked out the unit a few mornings ago, and I told her she needs a whole new AC system. It'll cost her fifteen grand."

"Fifteen grand?" If my trick to get more information worked once, maybe it'd work again.

"At least. That's just to bring the system up to code. Should've been done by the last owner, but it wasn't."

I pondered that for a moment. If Antonella was unwilling to replace the air-conditioning unit in her store, she must be running the business on a shoestring. A very thin shoestring, which she would come to regret once summertime rolled around.

"I thought the city made everyone get those energy-efficient units," I said. "At least, that's what I remember. Everyone told me I was lucky when I opened my store, because the Factory provides central air with our leases."

"They were right. Your friend should've rented a place out there too, but she probably got suckered into buying this old house. Everyone thinks these bungalows are such a steal, but they don't consider how much it costs to upgrade them. Take a look around. See all those wires?"

I glanced sideways. Instead of neatly hiding electrical wires behind drywall, someone had run paint-caked cords straight up the wall.

"Now that you mention it...it's not very pretty," I said.

"They were supposed to run the wire near the ground, so the furniture would hide it." He *tsk*ed a few times. "Can't believe this place ever passed code, to tell you the truth. Even back then."

"How old do you think this bungalow is? Twenty years?"

"Try almost forty," he said. "My guess is they built it in the eighties and no one ever thought to replace the electricity or air."

"So, what did my...um...friend ask you to do?"

Another shrug. "She wanted me to piecemeal it back together. We call it Southern engineering. A little duct tape, some bailing wire, you get the idea." He *tsked* yet again. "But on second thought, I don't think I can do it. It's too far gone. It's not worth the risk, and it'll never pass inspection. You tell your friend I'll be happy to install a brand-new system, and I'll even throw in a discount. But I can't patch this one back together again."

"I'll tell her. Thanks for being so honest."

"No problem." He moved over to where I stood to shake my hand once more, and I delicately placed my palm in his.

"And thanks for letting me tag along on your service call. I think I'm going to stay here for a bit and look for that...um...thing my friend needed."

"As long as your friend wouldn't mind, I guess it's okay with me. I have to head out to my next appointment, though." He finally released my hand, which somehow managed to stay clean. "Don't forget to pull the door shut behind you when you leave, so the lower lock catches in the latch. Tell your friend she'll need to engage the dead bolt with her key, though. And you tell that fiancé of yours he's one lucky guy."

"Will do."

The repairman retreated through the shop and disappeared into the parking lot. A sliver of sunshine splashed onto the linoleum floor as the door slowly closed behind him, and it stopped just shy of the threshold.

Now that I was alone, I could finally take my time and look around. While I didn't plan to touch anything, it couldn't hurt to scope out the competition, now, could it?

I started with the ceiling, where an antique chandelier, dripping with crystals, hung from a velvet cord. The fixture reminded me of a similar one I'd hung near the front door of Crowning Glory, but maybe that was just another coincidence.

Meanwhile, the walls around me held mirrored squares glued in a checkerboard pattern, which made the room seem bigger than it was. As a finishing touch, Antonella had flipped an old door on its side to create a front counter, where she placed a rusty cash register from the eighteen hundreds.

I moved over to the register and dusted off the nameplate, despite my best intentions not to touch anything. The plate read NATIONAL CASH REGISTER CO. in curlicue letters. My glance next fell on the counter underneath, where someone had shoved a piece of paper under the register's right side.

Only an inch of the page was visible under the machine, but the baby blue color seemed oddly familiar.

I pinched it between my thumb and forefinger and gently extracted it. The moment I spied the TIFFANY & CO logo at the top, I let out a tiny gasp.

It was the same ad Sabine d'Aulnay had brought to my studio Thursday. The one that showed an exquisite diamond tiara, which she wanted me to use as a headpiece for a one-of-a-kind bridal veil.

Not only that, but someone had x-ed through the phone number I'd scribbled on the ad. Now a new phone number appeared, along with a note: *She went to DuBois first. Give her 50 percent off.*

No wonder Sabine came back to my store yesterday and wanted her ad back! She must've found out about Antonella's shop and thought she could save money by hiring a less-experienced designer. Good luck with that. I could've told her. Why spend thousands of dollars on an intricate diamond tiara, only to have it paired with a basic veil?

There was no way Antonella had time to master the intricacies of French Chantilly lace, which was the finest lace available. A crown of diamonds deserved no less, and it deserved someone who knew how to work with it.

I could picture the look on Sabine's face when she lied to me yesterday. She'd gazed at me straight-faced and explained she needed to show the ad to her father. I'd doubted the explanation at the time, because I couldn't imagine why Christophe d'Aulnay would want to see a prototype for a wedding veil when he had so many other worries on his mind, but I'd let the comment pass.

Then again, what if Antonella had contacted Sabine, and not the other way around? Maybe she'd heard about Sabine's wedding through the grapevine and she'd urged the girl to switch shops.

No matter how it happened, neither of them had had the decency to give me a heads-up, which was downright underhanded.

I slowly returned the ad to its hiding place under the cash register. *If that's how they want to do business, they'll probably alienate half of Bleu Bayou. And the other half won't let them forget about it.*

Chapter 17

I turned away from the counter, my mind awhirl. Now that I knew what I was up against, it was time for me to do something about it.

The repairman had left the door to Antonella's shop cracked open, so I slipped through the exit and closed the door behind me before I made my way to the parking lot. Once I hopped into Ringo, my gaze automatically shifted to the passenger seat, where the cardboard tray with Ambrose's breakfast languished.

Oh, sugar. I'd forgotten all about it. If I didn't get home soon, the surprise would be ruined. Who wanted to eat a cold beignet, or drink an even-colder cup of coffee?

So, I drove back onto Highway 18 and pointed the car toward home. The road in front of me looked much different now. Where before I had the whole thing to myself, now I shared it with a pack of bicyclists who rode single file next to me. One of them wore a purple and gold LSU jersey that made him look like a plump harlequin, and he wobbled a bit as my car whooshed past him.

I arrived home in no time, and Ambrose met me at the front door. The minute he saw the carryall in my hand, his eyes lit up.

"Yeehaw." Gently, he took the breakfast tray from me. "To what do I owe the pleasure?"

"Let's just say it's payback for all the times you've spoiled me."

Like before, nothing stirred in the quiet as we made our way to the kitchen, and even the kiskadee outside my bedroom window had fallen silent. Which reminded me of something else.

"Hey, guess what?" I plopped onto the bench in our kitchen. "I bought a birdhouse yesterday for our backyard."

"Please tell me it's not pink." He placed the coffees on the farmhouse table, one by one, and then he jimmied the sack from its carrying case. "Just because I agreed to rent a pink house with you does *not* mean I like the color."

"Oops. My bad." I reached into the sack and pulled out a beignet, which still felt warm, praise the Lord. "At least it'll match the house, right?"

"Guess I'll make an exception. On account of the beignets and all." He withdrew one from the bag too, and took a hearty bite.

"Aha! I knew you'd be hungry after your long day yesterday."

He swallowed. "You were right. By the way…did you happen to see old what's-his-face while you were at the donut store?"

"Really? 'What's-his-face'? He has a name, you know." I took a bite of beignet too, before I set it aside. "I spoke with Grady, if that's what you mean. Nothing important, but he did mention Antonella's new store downtown."

"Did he tell you about the party?"

"Ambrose! You knew about the grand opening and you didn't tell me?" I swatted his arm playfully. "I thought we shared everything."

"Calm down. I only found out about it last night. Our favorite blogger came into my studio around dinnertime to drop off some flyers."

"You're kidding! She has a lot of nerve. Did you tell her off?"

"No, not really." Unfortunately, he took another bite, which meant I had to wait until he finished his mouthful to find out more. "I couldn't confront her right then because she was with the mayor. Did you know he rents out an office at the Factory too?"

"I do now. He told me about it yesterday. He said he used it as his campaign headquarters. But what was he doing with Antonella?" I tried to imagine the two of them standing in the middle of Ambrose's studio at twilight, thick as thieves, apparently.

"He was helping her distribute flyers for the grand opening. Look, it doesn't matter. She could hire the Times Square ball to drop out of the sky, but that doesn't mean people will go to her shop instead of yours. You have a great reputation, and no one knows her yet."

"Don't be too sure about that." My appetite had slowly waned, so I ignored the roll in front of me. "Remember that girl I told you about… Sabine d'Aulnay? The one who wanted me to make a veil for her diamond tiara? Well, apparently she has other ideas now."

"Other ideas?"

"It's true. I was in Antonella's hat shop this morning—"

"Whoa." His eyes widened. "Hold the phone. You were where?"

Uh-oh. I knew that tone. I was about to get a lecture on respecting other people's property. While part of me bristled, the other part knew he was right. "I know, I know. I had no right to be there. It just so happened an air-conditioner repairman showed up, and he let me in."

"Missy—"

"I only wanted to check out my hunch about the building permits. I promise, Ambrose. But there's no way a building inspector has been in there. He—or she—would never sign off on that mess. You should've seen the wires running up the walls."

Instead of lecturing me, Ambrose fell silent, which was twice as bad.

"I swear I didn't want to hurt anything," I quickly added. "I only wanted to look around. And that's where I found the Tiffany ad. It's the same ad Sabine showed me a few days ago, only now it's at Antonella's store."

"I get it." He didn't lecture me, but it was a close call. "But how is that Antonella's fault? It sounds like Sabine went looking for her, and not the other way around."

"That's what I thought at first. Until I saw a note Antonella wrote on the ad. She's giving Sabine a fifty-percent discount if she'll leave my studio and go to hers."

Finally, Ambrose's face untensed. "Well, that sucks."

"Tell me about it. And then there's—"

Just then, a ringtone shattered the quiet, and I automatically flinched.

"Cheese and crackers!" I scrambled to pull the phone from my pocket. "Remind me to turn that ringtone down. It scared the bejeebies out of me."

I quickly checked the caller ID, which showed a number for the Louisiana State Police Department. Only one person ever called me from that number: my best friend, Lance.

"Hi, Missy." He sounded wide awake, even at this early hour. "I'm glad you took my call."

"I always take your calls." I cupped my hand over the receiver and whispered Lance's name to Ambrose, before I returned to the line. "What's going on?"

"Hey…is that Ambrose in the background? Tell him I said hello."

"Lance says hello," I whispered, before I got back to the call. "Now, Lance. Are you going to tell me why you called, or do I have to guess?"

"Believe it or not, I've been at the police station all morning. We got a tip from someone who lives out on the bayou. She heard a noise the morning Ruby was murdered."

"You're kidding. What'd she say?"

"It was the lady who lives next door. She didn't want to call us at first—thought it was no big deal—but her husband convinced her she should. It happens all the time. People hear or see something strange, but they don't think anything of it. Then they can't get the memory out of their head, and it eats away at them until they finally give us a ring."

I swiveled around on the bench. I hadn't thought about Ruby since yesterday afternoon, when Hollis came by my studio. "Are you going over the police report?"

I could picture him sitting at his desk with an enormous pile of file folders in front of him, some as tall as his shoulder.

"I am. I'm trying to connect the dots. Apparently, this neighbor heard Ruby's dog barking the morning she was murdered."

"You mean Jacques? You know that dog's a menace, right?"

"Yeah, that's what she said." He didn't sound like he quite believed me. "I didn't run into the dog last night, so I wouldn't know."

"That's right… I forgot you spent the night at Hollis's place. But I don't see how a barking dog is any big deal. From what I've seen, Jacques barks all the time."

"That wasn't all she heard. She heard a man's voice too. Someone yelled at the dog to shut up. It happened just after sunrise."

"Interesting." I touched Ambrose's arm to get his attention. When he glanced over, I nodded at the living room, where I intended to head next. "So, your caller heard the ruckus first thing in the morning. And, come to think of it, the dog doesn't usually bark until someone steps onto his dock." I slowly rose, and then I walked away from the kitchen.

"What time did you get to Ruby's house that day?" he asked.

"Hmm…let me think." Although I'd visited Ruby's mobile home only two days ago, it seemed like a lifetime had passed. "We probably got there around ten."

"Are you sure?"

"Um, hm." I remembered chastising Hollis about waking up so late. Especially since Beatrice and I had been working for two whole hours by then. "Hollis was still sleeping when we got there. I gave him a hard time about it."

Once I entered the living room, I made a beeline for the overstuffed couch and sat.

"I'm going to ask Hollis if he heard the noise that morning, but my guess is that he's a heavy sleeper."

"He is. And he didn't say anything about it to me yesterday." I heard a soft scratching noise over the receiver. "Are you writing down notes?"

"Of course. It's all part of the police report. So, where was the dog when you got there Thursday?"

"He was on the shoreline. Beatrice tossed him a bone so he wouldn't attack us. Thank goodness it worked."

"Did anything seem out of place to you?"

"No, not really." I could picture the two of us on the dock, but nothing seemed strange. A soft breeze blew through the tupelos; that much I remembered. And the dog went crazy for the rawhide bone. Nothing unusual there. "The dog growled at me at first, like he always does. But once Beatrice tossed him the bone, he forgot all about me."

I shifted onto another couch cushion. Halfway there, my hip landed against something soft and squishy, so I reached for it. It was the Nerf football Ambrose and Hollis had tossed back and forth the other night.

The ball obviously didn't belong to Ambrose, since jagged teeth marks sliced through the foam. It had to belong to Hollis, or, more likely, Jacques.

"You said you're going to call Hollis?"

"Yeah, when it gets a little later. I put the stingray device on his phone, but he didn't get any strange calls last night. And I requested a backup unit to patrol the woods, just in case."

"You're going to leave him by himself today?" I knew the answer, but I didn't like it.

"I have to. I've got to follow up on this lead. Don't worry...he'll be fine. My backup won't let anything bad happen to him."

"That's not it." I carefully palmed the football. "I just hate the thought of Hollis being out there by himself. It's got to get lonely."

"He's a big boy, Missy. He'll be okay."

"I know. But still..." The foam squished beneath my fingertips, which gave me an idea. "Maybe I'll go see him this morning. He forgot something at my house, and I could return it. That way, he won't think I'm checking up on him."

"It sounds like something you'd do." He chuckled knowingly. "But watch your step when you're out there. I'll tell my backup you're coming, so she can keep an eye out for you."

"Thanks. And good luck with your tip. I hope it pans out."

Once I clicked off the line, I slid the cell back in my pocket. Then I tucked the football behind my back and made my way to the kitchen. Ambrose had finished his breakfast by now, and tufts of powdered sugar dusted the table in front of him.

"How's Lance?" he asked, as soon as I plopped onto the bench next to him.

"He's okay. He's back at the police station, working on a tip from a neighbor."

"Anything important?"

"Hard to say." I worried my lower lip as I thought things through. "Too bad he had to leave Hollis all alone today. I'm not good with it, to tell you the truth."

"I'm sure he'll be fine. If I know Lance, he asked for some backup out there."

"He did. But that's not the point. I think Hollis should be with people he knows today. His grandma only died two days ago."

"That's true. But he might think you're trying to babysit him if you go out there. I remember what it was like to be eighteen. You think you're invincible."

"I'm one step ahead of you." I slowly withdrew the football from behind my back and plunked it on the table. "I'll tell him I went over to return this."

"A football?" He didn't seem as impressed with my plan as I'd hoped.

"Why not? I'll tell him I thought he might want to toss the ball around with Jacques today. Look at those teeth marks."

"It's a stretch, but he might buy it." He dusted his hands over the tabletop, and even more sugar rained down. "Anyway, there's no chance I'm letting you go out there alone. Give me a few minutes to shower and change."

"You don't have to do that. I know you're swamped with catalog work. And Lance said the backup unit will be watching the house. I'm sure we'll be fine."

Ambrose playfully snatched the football from me. "You can talk until you're blue in the face, but it won't change anything. I'm going with you... like it or not."

"If that's the case...I guess I like it."

"Good." He smiled as he rose from the table. "No telling what we'll find out there today, but at least you'll learn how to throw a decent lateral."

Chapter 18

We arrived on the bayou fifteen minutes later, once Ambrose had had a chance to shower and change.

He slowed the Audi to a crawl as we passed an especially thick clump of kudzu on the path to Ruby's house.

"There's the backup unit." He pointed to a white police cruiser partially hidden by the dense foliage.

"Lance must've told her about us. Otherwise, she'd make us stop."

Sure enough, the cruiser didn't budge, and we arrived at the mobile home a few seconds later. Ambrose pulled the Audi behind the listing dock and switched off the ignition.

"Did you remember another rawhide?" He grabbed the football and stepped out of the car.

"You bet. A couple of 'em." I patted the bulge in my pocket before I threw open the door and stepped outside.

The moment my feet hit hardpacked mud, nature sounds surrounded me. The constant buzz of cicadas in the bushes provided one long whole note, while nearby bullfrogs added bass half-notes of their own. *Hhhooonnnkkk.*

Along with the wildlife, a soft *whoosh* of rustling leaves sounded overhead as the breeze flowed through the tupelos. Although I didn't spy Jacques yet, I suspected the dog was hiding behind one of the pilings on the dock. "Here we go again." I slowly withdrew the dog treat from my pocket. "Let's hope it works as good as last time."

I thrust the rawhide in front of me and cautiously stepped onto the dock. I felt like a penitent, coming to lay an offering at the foot of the Virgin Mary in her baby-blue rock grotto.

Two steps in, something moved in front of me.

"*Bonjour*, Jacques," I said, just as Beatrice had done. "I brought *déjeuner!*"

I cautiously moved forward with the dog's breakfast, the planks groaning beneath my feet. The noise flushed out the dog, who'd been squatting behind the very last piling. Dull leaves and green slime matted the animal's fur.

"Who's a good boy?" I said, in a singsong voice.

"That's the monster you've been telling me about?" Ambrose spoke behind me, and he sounded amused. "He doesn't look so bad. He needs a bath, but he doesn't look like a man-eater."

"Just you wait. Heaven help us if we run out of rawhides." I cautiously took a few more steps, the planks groaning again. "Thatta boy. Here you go."

Still skittish from my last run-in, I tossed the bone a few yards from the dog's snout. After sniffing it a few times, he trotted forward and snatched it in his teeth. Then he languidly returned to his hiding spot on the edge of the dock.

"Whew!" I said. "Thank goodness he can be bribed with food."

"I still think you're exaggerating," Ambrose didn't sound impressed. "He probably just wanted to play with you the other day."

"Yeah, that's right. He's sweet like that." Hopefully, a bit of the sarcasm would come through. "He's just an overgrown puppy."

With one problem fixed, now I needed to find Hollis. My gaze traveled to the mobile home, where a faded calico curtain had been pulled tight across the front window. Not only that, but the porch light still cast an eerie blue glow on the rickety steps, which told me no one had been outside today.

"I'll bet you anything Hollis is still asleep," I said. "Wonder if he even knows the morning's half over?"

"Probably not. He probably doesn't care either."

Before I could speak again, a low growl sounded in the distance, and this time it had nothing to do with the dog on the dock. It sounded like the blades of an enormous fan churning through the air. Either that, or a giant mosquito buzzed over the waterline.

"What the—?" Ambrose asked.

The noise grew louder by the second. When the dog finally noticed it, he dropped the half-eaten treat to the ground to gaze at the water.

Wwwhhhiiirrr. By now, the sound filled the air. The mechanical noise ebbed and flowed, just like the small waves that lapped along the shoreline.

The next thing I heard was a bullhorn, of all things. It broadcast a man's voice over the high-pitched whir, loud and clear. "Take a look to your right, folks, and you'll see one of the original houses out here on the bayou. That home has been here since the nineteen forties. Come back in a few months and it'll look a whole lot different."

The upturned nose of an airboat emerged from around the bend. It was a ruby red boat with forest green trim, wide enough to sit at least three people side by side.

The boat skimmed over the water, propelled by a giant fan attached to its stern. The boat's driver perched in a metal chair high above the deck, like the lookout on a pirate ship.

"I can guess who owns that boat," I yelled to Ambrose. "It's painted just like the *Riverboat Queen*."

"Really? That's weird." Ambrose raised his voice too, which caught the attention of the dog.

By now, Jacques had been the only one not making noise, so he decided to bark at the approaching airboat for all he was worth.

Miraculously, nothing stirred inside the mobile home. While I expected the front door to crash open at any second, it didn't happen.

The bullhorn clicked on again. "There are only a few properties like this left. These people grew up on the bayou, eating gators and frogs' legs and anything else that moved. When I get my hands on the property..." The churning fan blades drowned out the next few words, as the boat pulled closer to the dock.

"What'd he say?" I yelled to Ambrose.

"He said something about getting his hands on the property."

"He can't say that! He has no idea what's going to happen to it."

After a moment, the guide finally noticed we were standing on the shore, and he lowered the bullhorn. Sure enough, it was Christophe d'Aulnay... all five feet, five inches of him.

"Greetings, friends!" Not surprisingly, he didn't really need the bullhorn, because his voice boomed across the water. "*Bonjour*."

Our exchange seemed to pique the interest of his passengers, and several lifted their cell phones to snap a picture of the strangers on the shore.

"What do they want us to do?" I asked in a stage whisper. "Tap-dance?"

"Beats me." Ambrose shrugged as he thought it over. "I guess they think we live here. Act like we're natives."

He started to wave his arms in the air like a madman, until I shushed him. "Stop that! They'll think we're crazy."

"Let 'em. I don't care," he said.

By now, the boat had drawn even closer to the dock, which drove the dog wild. Jacques ended up spinning around in circles like a whirling dervish.

Once the boat reached the edge of the planks, the driver cut the motor, and the fan blades slowly ground to a halt.

"What're you doing here, Captain?" I called, when the noise finally dimmed.

"We always stop here on our tour." As always, the man spoke much too loudly. "I like to give my customers a taste for how people out here live."

"Does Hollis know you come out here?" It seemed to me the teen might have a few choice words to say about being included in Captain Christophe's riverboat tours.

"*Tot ce que.* Whatever. Since we're on the river, there's not a whole lot he can do about it. Now, is there?"

While I didn't want to make a scene, I also didn't like the captain's attitude. He acted like he already owned Ruby's property, which couldn't be further from the truth.

"Why do you say that?" I yelled. "This is all Hollis's property. Not yours."

"Not yet anyway," he yelled back to me. "Okay, folks. Say good-bye to our friends. It's time to move along."

I was about to say more when the driver suddenly switched on the engine and the giant fan blades roared to life. Within moments, the sound of metal slicing through air eclipsed everything else on the bayou.

"Well, he has a lot of nerve," I said, once the boat slipped around the bend again.

"You're right. Guess he thinks he can do anything he wants out here because he's Christophe d'Aulnay."

"That's not all, Bo." I cast a worried glance back at the dock, where Jacques had flopped down in a heap. "I've got a funny feeling the captain already knows something we don't."

Chapter 19

A few moments later, the door to the mobile home finally swung open, and Hollis stuck his head out.

"What's going on?" He sounded sleepy, and his hair stuck out in all directions, like the quills on a fair-haired porcupine.

"Captain d'Aulnay came by," I explained. "He brought a boatload of tourists over here."

"He what?"

"He said he always includes your grandma's house on his river tours. It's to give his customers a look at how the locals"—I flicked my fingers a few times in the air to indicate quote marks—"live around here. Whatever that means."

"He can't do that," Hollis said. "Can he?"

"'Fraid so." Ambrose had turned toward the mobile home too. "He can do pretty much anything he wants out on the river. The waterways are fair game."

"Whaddya know. Say…do you guys wanna come inside?" Hollis asked.

"We'd love to." I answered for Ambrose too, since the meeting with the captain had left me discombobulated. I wanted nothing more than to sit down for a few minutes and think.

Bo moved toward the stairs first, the football tucked tight by his side.

"Wait for me!" I hurried to catch up, since there was no telling when Jacques would revive. While I pitied the poor dog, nothing said I had to spend any more time with him than necessary. Who knew a dog's tongue could stretch out that far?

Once I climbed the stairs, I stepped through the shredded screen door and entered the living room. It took a second for my eyes to adjust to the dim light. Nothing had changed inside, as far as I could tell. Over there, on the flowered couch, sat the puddle of newspapers I'd somehow managed to wrangle into a pile. On top of it was the letter of intent from Remy Gaudet, which Ruby may, or may not, have read before she died.

I followed Hollis into the kitchen, which was sunny and cheerful by comparison. "Lance came over here last night, right?"

"Yeah. We hung out and watched some football."

My gaze fell to the pine picnic table, where the drawing of the bell curve still sat. I'd used the curve to explain supply and demand to Hollis, and it hadn't moved since Thursday. "Hard to believe I was here only two days ago."

"I know." Hollis's gaze followed mine. "I tried to look at your notes again. I really did. But I couldn't concentrate."

"Of course you couldn't." I sat on the bench by the picnic table, while Hollis leaned against the kitchen counter. Ambrose must've gotten waylaid in the living room, because he didn't join us.

"By the way," I asked, "did you have a chance to call your grandma's sister and tell her about what happened?"

Hollis nodded. "Yeah. She's coming out for the funeral. We're gonna have it on Monday. You can come, right?"

"We wouldn't miss it." Ambrose wouldn't mind if I spoke for him again, since he'd want to be there as much as I did.

"Good." Hollis sounded relieved. "The guy at the funeral home helped me pick out a coffin and stuff. And lots of people said they're gonna come to the funeral. Guess Grandma had more friends than I thought."

Uh-oh. He's right. Half the town probably will show up. "Say, Hollis. Did the funeral director mention anything about a reception afterward?"

"A what?"

I winced, since he had no idea what I was talking about. "There's usually a reception after a funeral. We have to think about what to serve everyone. It doesn't have to be fancy, but you should probably offer people cookies and punch, at least."

"You mean I have to feed all those people? I don't—"

"Hold on." While I didn't like to interrupt him, I also didn't want him to panic. "I'll make a few phone calls this afternoon. I'm sure everybody would love to help you. No one expects you to do everything by yourself."

"Thanks. I don't know about any of that stuff. I've only been to one funeral and I was, like, in kindergarten."

"Let me take care of it. As a matter of fact, I know someone who might be able to do the whole thing." The minute I'd mentioned food, the thought of Miss Odilia's Southern Eatery popped into my head. She'd know what to make for the funeral, and she could feed any sized crowd. "I'll bet Odilia LaPorte would love to help out."

"She's the lady who let me borrow the jacket at her restaurant, right?"

"That's her. I'll call her later today and get everything all set up."

Now that he'd been thrown a lifeline, Hollis's breathing grew normal again. Earlier, it'd come in fits and starts, and I worried I might have to revive the teen right there on the kitchen floor.

"Thanks again, Miss DuBois. You're the best."

"Who's the best?" Ambrose wandered into the kitchen, apparently finished with whatever he was doing in the front room.

"We were just talking about the funeral," I said. "It's going to be Monday, and Hollis asked us both to be there."

"Of course we'll come." Ambrose didn't hesitate. "What about afterward?"

"We were talking about that too," I said. "I'm going to call Miss Odilia and see if she'll bring the food. Knowing her, I don't even have to ask."

"You're right. Say, Hollis." Ambrose moved over to where the teen stood by the sink. "I heard someone called you yesterday and tried to threaten you. Did they ever call back?"

"Nah. At least I don't think so. I probably wouldn't hear it if they called when I was sleeping anyway. I don't hear anything then."

"So, you *are* a heavy sleeper. I knew it." While I knew he liked to sleep late, I only guessed Hollis also slept like a log. And that reminded me of something else Lance had said during our phone call. "One of your neighbors gave Detective LaPorte a tip this morning."

Hollis squinted. "A tip?"

"She called the police department and said Jacques was going crazy the morning your grandma died."

Recognition sparked behind his eyes. "I'll bet you anything it was old Miss Lucy. She's been here a billion years, and she hates Jacques."

"She didn't call to complain," I quickly added, "but to tell him something else. She heard Jacques first, but then she heard a man shouting at your dog to stay quiet."

"That's what she said?"

"Yeah. I guess Jacques surprised the guy, so he started yelling."

"I don't get it," Hollis said. "Most people around here know Jacques, and they know to watch out for him."

Before I could say more, the cell phone in my pocket began to vibrate. I tried to grab it before the ringer exploded, but soon the kitchen filled with the sound of Harry Connick Jr.

"Sweet baby Jesus." I shoved my hand in my pocket and whipped out the noisemaker. I also shot Ambrose a recriminating glance, since he'd promised to remind me to turn the darn thing down.

"Oh yeah," Ambrose said with a grin, "you're supposed to fix the volume."

"Thanks. Thanks a lot." I quickly accepted the call, which silenced the ringer. "Hello. This is Missy DuBois."

"Oh, thank God!" It was a woman's voice, and she sounded clearly relieved to be speaking with me.

"Can I help you?"

"I sure hope so. It's me, Missy…Sabine d'Aulnay. Do you remember me?"

"Uh, yeah." *How could I forget?* While that's what I wanted to say, it didn't seem very polite, or very wise, at the moment. "Of course I remember you. How can I help you today?"

"I've made a terrible mistake." She lowered her voice a few notches. "I need to see you right away. This can't wait."

"You mean now?" I glanced at the cat-shaped clock, where the long paw stretched toward eleven and the short paw rested on twelve. At this rate, I'd never finish my errands by noon. "I…I guess so. Can you tell me what's going on, though?"

"I can't talk right now. But I'll explain when we get together. I can be at your shop in ten minutes. Will that work?"

I brought my gaze from the clock to Ambrose. While I didn't want to leave him, Sabine sounded panicked. And I knew he'd take care of Hollis, so I wouldn't have to worry about that.

"I guess I can meet you," I said. "Let's make it fifteen minutes, though, so I can wrap up things over here."

"Great! I'll see you then."

As soon as she clicked off the line, I slid the cell back in my pocket. "There's been a change in plans, gentlemen. This day keeps getting stranger and stranger."

Chapter 20

Ambrose didn't look surprised by my announcement. "I figured something was up."

Slowly, I rose from the bench. The room didn't seem nearly as bright, or as comfortable now, since I'd been asked to leave it. "Remember Sabine d'Aulnay?"

"Yeah. She was your problem client, right?"

I hesitated before answering. It wasn't polite to criticize clients in public—although this one surely deserved it—and Hollis was listening in, after all.

"Let's just say we've had our disagreements. I'm afraid she wants me to meet her back at Crowning Glory."

"That's okay." Hollis didn't look surprised by my news either. "You go ahead if you need to leave. I don't mind."

"But what about you, Bo?" I asked. "Do you care if I go?"

"I'll miss you, if that's what you mean. But I understand." He pulled out the keys to the Audi, which he tossed to me. "Here. You take my car. And don't worry about Hollis and me. We'll be fine." He patted the football's laces, which gave me a pretty good idea of what the guys would be doing while I was away.

"Great." I gave him a quick kiss on the cheek as I passed the sink. "I'll call you when I find out what she wants. And thanks for letting me use your car."

I waved good-bye, and then I moved into the living room. At the last second, I remembered the leftover rawhide in my pocket, which I'd no doubt need to toss to Jacques before I left the property.

"See you soon!" I yelled over my shoulder as I stepped outside.

The dog had disappeared again, but I kept one eye on the dock, nevertheless. His modus operandi seemed to involve hiding behind a tree or crouching next to a weathered piling and then jumping out at his unsuspecting victim. No wonder he'd surprised the visitor on Thursday.

"Here, Jacques!" I approached the dock. Better to head him off at the pass than become his next victim.

After a minute, the familiar *click-clack* of the dog's nails on hardwoods rang out as he padded down the dock. I tossed him the rawhide, which he once more grabbed before he retreated to his hiding spot. *Amazing.* That dog could appear and disappear like a vapor, even with the telltale click of his toenails.

I hopped into the Audi and sped away, my thoughts a million miles away. Thank goodness Ambrose had chosen to stay behind with Hollis. What if the crazy caller made a repeat performance and tried to get in touch with him again?

Or, worse yet, what if the caller decided to deliver the message in person this time? True, Lance had stationed a backup officer nearby, but suspects had been known to skirt around a police officer at the scene of a crime.

As a matter of fact, not long ago, Lance told me about a particular thief he'd run across. This man liked to hang around a house after he'd burglarized it, just so he could watch the faces of his victims when they discovered they'd been robbed. He'd sneak away from the property to stash his loot and then return to gawk at the chaos he'd caused. That was when I realized how evil some people could be.

I shuddered and forced myself to think about something else. Something like Sabine d'Aulnay. Why in the world would the girl call me only one day after she came to my shop to ask for her Tiffany ad back? What did she want from me now? To tell me she was taking her business elsewhere, which I already knew?

By the time I mulled that question a bit, I'd arrived at the Factory. Most of the parking lot sat empty, since lots of the shops had closed for the weekend. Brides and their maids could drop in anytime they wanted Monday through Friday, but Saturdays usually required an appointment.

A powder-blue Thunderbird convertible had the entire front row to itself, so I pulled up next to it. The car's license plate read POLITICO, which gave me a pretty good idea of whom it belonged to. Not only that, but I recalled Mayor Turcott and his assistant heading to a similar car yesterday when I stopped them to speak to the mayor.

Our new mayor obviously had excellent taste in both cars and clothes. I passed by the gleaming, sloped hood of the convertible as I made my way to Crowning Glory. Outside of a few banged-up delivery vans and FedEx trucks, I didn't spot anything that would pass for Sabine's car, which meant I'd arrived before her.

Come to think of it…nothing said I had to be early for our appointment, and it might do her a world of good to have to wait on other people for a change.

Besides, this might be my one and only chance to speak with the mayor without his assistant eavesdropping. So, I turned around and began to walk back the way I'd come. I could tell Mayor Turcott all about Antonella's new shop, since I'd seen it only yesterday, and I could relay what the repairman had to say. I'd never forgive myself if a fire broke out in that shop and I hadn't done a thing to prevent it.

That was the excuse I gave myself, anyway, as I made my way across the parking lot. After a moment, I arrived at the sparkling glass atrium that bisected the Factory.

Like always, sunlight glanced off the walls of glass and lit the interior, although the air inside felt cool and comfortable, once I entered the building. Two Mies van der Rohe couches faced the front door, neither of them occupied. Ditto for some modern chairs placed catty-corner to the couches. I rode up to the second floor in the building's elevator, where it deposited me at the start of a long hall.

Here a decorator had framed old labels from produce crates and hung them on the walls. The Factory produced hot sauce back in its heyday, so many of the labels featured fat red peppers with curly green stems. One showed an artfully shaded burlap bag that overflowed with pepper seeds, while the last one in the bunch showcased an apple-cheeked sun smiling above a rolling field.

The cheeky sun blurred in my periphery as I walked. Two separate studios anchored the far end of the hall: Pink Cake Boxes, the bakery owned by Bettina LeBlanc, and one that used to belong to Happily Ever After, a special events company. I'd always loved the name of that company, even if the sentiment didn't exactly describe what happened to one of the businesses' owners.

No, that person died tragically young, and the other, a cousin, sold the business soon afterward. Now, a shiny new brass nameplate announced the offices of Zephirin A. Turcott, Mayor and Attorney at Law.

A sliver of light pooled under the door, so I cautiously knocked. I didn't really expect a response, though, since I doubted a receptionist would work on the weekend. After a moment, I nudged the door open and stepped inside.

The change was dramatic. Where before, the offices of Happily Ever After featured whitewashed furniture and pastel scenes from famous fairy tales on the walls, the remodeled office held heavy, dark antiques and staid pictures of English hunting parties. A massive mahogany bookcase lorded over a far wall, and some decidedly uncomfortable-looking straight-back chairs had been placed in front of it.

I eyed the bookcase first. It contained the usual knickknacks for an office like this, a Waterford clock balanced on a foot-high stack of leather-bound books, a fake fern potted in a blue-and-white Chinese porcelain bowl, and a row of textbooks, probably for show, since the spines hadn't been cracked.

I stepped closer to the books, which turned out to be a full set of the *Classics of International Law.* Once I determined that, I bypassed the rest of the books and moved to a door on the other side of the bookcase. Unlike the other one, this door was ajar, so I cautiously pushed it open and squeezed through the entrance.

Nothing stirred back here either. At one time, Charlotte Deveraux, a popular wedding planner, had worked in the office on the right, but now it looked dark and shuttered. The other office, on the left, used to house her cousin, Paxton Haney, and that door stood wide open.

I moved closer to the open office and peeked around the door frame. Sure enough, this space looked completely different too. Gone were the overflowing file cabinets and birch furniture, replaced by an ornately carved mahogany desk, an equally somber bookcase, and a Tiffany lamp with a multicolored shade.

I expected to find the mayor somewhere inside, since the kaleidoscope lampshade glowed, but he wasn't. *Dagnabbit!* Just when I was about to leave, the faint *whoosh* of running water sounded through the wall.

Aha! The men's room. I knew from past experience this office shared a wall with the bathroom, and that must be where the mayor had gone.

I set my sights on a richly padded armchair tucked under the lip of the mahogany desk. I pulled the chair away from the desk, but it bumped into a trash can and knocked the thing over. The brass trash can spilled a river of detritus—wadded-up legal papers, a few used tissues, and an amber canister—out into the open.

I quickly bent to clean up my mess. Once I grabbed the papers, I reached for the canister, but it rolled away. A little more stretching, though, and I managed to grasp the bottle between my thumb and forefinger, before I straightened.

It was a prescription bottle, of all things. When I shook it, a few pills clacked together. It also bore a label on its front, but someone had x-ed through the patient's name with a thick, black Sharpie. The rest of the label was intact, and it gave the name of the medicine—Xanax—along with the prescribed dosage, which was pegged at two milligrams.

Sweet mother of pearl! I nearly dropped it to the floor. Didn't Xanax mirror lorazepam, which was the drug the ME assumed had been given to Ruby before she died? Apparently, the prescription came from the Shoprite Deluxe here in Bleu Bayou, and it'd been filled only a few days ago.

How could someone blow through that many tablets in only three days? Not only that, but why was the patient's name removed, as if it held some deep, dark secret that even the trash hauler wasn't supposed to see?

I slowly retrieved my cell phone, since every instinct told me to call Lance. He'd been the one to let me know about the medical examiner's findings, and he'd know what to do next.

Thank goodness I kept the number for the Louisiana State Police Department on my speed dial. Before I could punch the button, though, something squeaked nearby, and it sounded suspiciously like the handle of a paper towel dispenser on the other side of the wall.

Hell's bells! I yelped and quickly shoved the bottle back in the trash can. Then I kicked the can under the chair and dove for the seat cushion.

I landed on it just as the mayor appeared behind me.

"What the—"

"Hello, Mayor Turcott." I quickly rose from the chair and whirled around. "I saw your car in the parking lot, so I knew you'd be here today."

I offered him my hand, which he shook after first wiping his palm on the leg of his trousers. Even on a Saturday, the mayor was dressed to the nines, with a navy Lacoste polo tucked into dressy gray slacks.

He recovered amazingly fast. "What a pleasant surprise. How very nice to see you today." He was obviously lying, and we both knew it. "And what can I do for you, Miss DuBois?"

"I wanted to tell you more about the new hat shop. You know…Goode Hat-i-tudes. There's…um…something wrong with the wiring in that place."

His smile slipped a bit. "Hmmm. I see. Is that what you're really concerned about, or does this have something to do with another competitor coming to town? If that's the case, you don't have to worry. Antonella's a good sport, and I'm sure there's plenty of business to go around."

I couldn't help but notice he'd used her first name. This was going to be even harder than I thought. Not only that, but the cell phone was burning a hole in my pocket, since I longed to call Lance and tell him about the prescription bottle.

"I never gave a thought to the competition from her," I lied. In all fairness, he started it by saying he was happy to see me, when he wasn't. "While I'm not crazy about the thought of another hat store opening up around here, I'm more worried about what's going to happen to her customers."

"Really? It sounds like sour grapes to me." By now his smile had completely vanished. "Unless you have hard evidence to show something's wrong with Antonella's store, it's only gossip. And I don't trade in gossip."

I hesitated, but only for an instant. If I didn't speak now, I never would. "I know it sounds like sour grapes, sir. But I was in the building yesterday with a repairman. He told me the air-conditioning unit there needs to come out, because it's that unstable."

"Then I guess it's a good thing we're in the month of October. She probably won't have to use it at all. Now, if you don't mind, I really do have to get back to work."

Apparently, he was willing to forgive Antonella for any and all trespasses, even if it meant putting her customers at risk. His ties to the Goode family must run even deeper than I thought.

"You're not even going to send an inspector over there?" I asked.

"Not on a Saturday, I'm not. And we have the grand opening in two days. I think we all could use a little celebration around here. Especially after everything that's happened lately."

He must be talking about the murders. Over the past two years, Bleu Bayou had faced more than its fair share of crime. At last count, four people had been murdered in the antebellum homes around here, which was an ungodly amount for such a small town.

"I'm not against us having a celebration, but I think it's premature."

"What do you want me to do, Miss DuBois? Postpone the party? Is that it?"

"Yes. It doesn't have to be forever. Just long enough for her to fix some things in her shop. That's all. Something every business owner should do anyway."

The more I spoke, the more convinced I became. No shop owner should be allowed to skirt the rules, no matter how influential or "generous"—his word, not mine—the girl's family was.

"Let me think about it." His offhand manner told me he never would. "Now, if you don't mind...I have work to do. What with the party on Monday, I have a thousand details to manage and no assistant today."

He nodded to the open door, just in case I didn't catch his drift the first time.

Yep...he's dismissing me, all right. I could either waste my time and breath trying to convince him otherwise, or I could take what was left of my dignity and leave. Which would give me just enough time to call Lance before Sabine arrived at my hat studio.

Given the rough day, and the horrible week, I'd had, it wasn't a hard choice to make.

Chapter 21

I slowly rose from the chair. After offering the mayor a perfunctory handshake, I numbly retreated to the outer office.

My head was spinning from our encounter. First came the unexpected discovery of the pill bottle in his trash can, followed by his confirmation that money meant more to him than the law, which was something I already suspected.

I mulled over our conversation as I passed the framed artwork and rode the elevator down one floor, where the car's doors *swooshed* open on the quiet lobby.

It took me a lot longer to leave the glass pyramid than it had to enter it. By the time I made my way to Crowning Glory, my gaze still lowered, I felt more confused than ever. I barely noticed someone was waiting for me outside my studio, until I suddenly heard my name.

"Hi, Missy."

I glanced up to see Sabine d'Aulnay, who wore black Lululemon leggings today and a simple pink Rag & Bone sweater. Gone was the over-the-top St. John suit, or the enormous Louis Vuitton handbag that nearly upended Beatrice's coffee cup yesterday.

"Hello, Sabine."

The girl automatically checked her Rolex, which sparkled in the noon sun. "You're a little bit late again, but that's okay."

"Sorry about that. I had business on the other end of the building."

I quickly thrust my key into the shop's front door, and then I waited for Sabine to walk into the room ahead of me.

In place of the Vuitton, she carried a burlap bookbag, which she swung over her shoulder as she made her way through the shop. "Thanks for meeting me today," she called over her shoulder.

"No problem. What can I do for you?" I still had a sour taste in my mouth from the conversation with the mayor, and I didn't relish the thought of hearing Sabine's backhanded compliments again, if she chose to lob them my way.

"Do you remember this?" She'd taken one of the bar stools by the counter, and she carefully withdrew the Tiffany ad from her bookbag.

"Is that the same ad I saw yesterday?" I moved to the other bar stool and pretended to study it. "You told me you wanted to show it to your dad. What happened?"

"Here's the thing." She dropped her gaze, while she pretended to study the picture too. "I never meant to show it to my father."

"You didn't?" *At least she's not lying anymore.* "But you said you wanted to get his opinion."

"Look, I haven't been very honest with you."

"Really?" I finally gave in to the urge to repay all her backhanded compliments. I couldn't help myself, to be honest. "Bless your heart." *Boy, does that feel good.* "But why would you lie to me?"

"Because I was worried you might overcharge me. I asked someone else to give an estimate on what it'd cost to make my veil. Someone I thought would be cheaper."

"You don't say. You know, you could've told me you wanted a second opinion. I would've been happy to give you some references."

"But I didn't know that's how this stuff works." Instead of looking at me now, she began to worry the ad with her thumb, and before long, she'd rolled one of the corners into a tiny wave. "I thought you wouldn't work with me if you knew I went behind your back."

"It would've been nice if you would've told me."

"To be honest, people always overcharge me when I order something." Finally, she looked up from the paper wave, her forehead creased with worry. "People hear my last name, and the next thing you know, the price doubles."

Wait a minute, I wanted to say. What about the expensive sunbonnets you picked out for your bridesmaids? That was your choice, not theirs. No wonder people overcharge you, when you say things like "money's no object." But this time, I kept my tongue in check.

"I thought maybe you'd do the same thing to me. You know, take advantage of my name. Guess I was wrong."

"Why? What did your second source say?"

"She told me she'd give me a big discount, on account of how she's new and all." Sabine chuckled, but it was bitter. "Some discount! She wanted five thousand dollars, and that didn't include the fittings. Those cost a hundred dollars a pop, and she said I'd need at least four of them."

"Holy-schmoly!" I quickly calculated the sum. "She wanted fifty-four hundred dollars for a simple veil, when she didn't even have to make the headpiece?" While I didn't want to gloat—okay, maybe a little—Antonella's store would never survive if she charged people that much.

Who knew what she based her prices on? Maybe she looked at my rates and thought she could charge the same. Little did she know I only charged half as much when I first started out.

"I guess I blew it." Sabine had gone back to studying the ad.

"Look...there's no harm done. Why don't we pretend like it never happened. Hello. I'm Melissa DuBois."

Finally, she gave a real chuckle. "That sounds good. But there's one more thing I need to tell you. Only, you've got to swear you won't repeat it."

"Cross my heart," I said.

"Okay, then." She took a deep breath. "My father's not paying for my wedding anymore. He can't. He said his business is going bankrupt."

Shut my mouth and call me Shirley! Could it be that one of the richest families in Bleu Bayou had gone belly-up? "Come again?"

"It's true. My dad said he can't afford to pay for the wedding. I have to pay for everything myself. All of it."

"You poor thing." I racked my brain for an appropriate response. When none came, I settled on the one thing we Southerners always said when words fail us. "Can I get you a cold drink?"

"No, that's okay. I'm not thirsty. I can't even have the wedding on the *Riverboat Queen*, because it's already booked that day." She looked miserable now. Or, about as miserable as a housecat in a rainstorm, as my grandfather used to say.

"I...I had no idea. I'm so sorry."

Finally, she glanced up again. "Me too. It's not anyone's fault. Dad said it's just the way things are right now. He can't expand his business because he doesn't have anywhere else to put more boats."

"But he's got the airboat doing tours. And what about the *Riverboat Queen*? That thing's huge."

"That's the problem. It's too big to make it through the small waterways. And one airboat out there isn't gonna cut it. He said he needs at least three more boats and another dock."

"Hmmm." I dropped my gaze to the Tiffany ad. She'd definitely worried the corner to a nubbin, and it hung from the page by a thread. "You know, you've got your heart set on a very expensive tiara. Maybe we should look at some other options."

"I already thought of that. I know I can't afford this one anymore. At least, not a real one."

"Hey, that's a good idea. Why don't you ask your jeweler to make a fake one? Those Swarovski crystals sparkle just like the real thing."

"They do?" she asked.

"Yep. They shine like nobody's business when you use enough of them."

"I don't suppose…" She left the question unasked. She seemed to want my help again, only she didn't know how to ask for it.

"And I'd love to work on your project again." I saved her the trouble. "I could even set up a payment plan, so you don't have to pay for the whole deposit up front."

"That'd be great! Dad said it's only a temporary setback. He's trying to buy some land around here, only he's had a hard time with the seller."

"Why? Where's he looking?"

"He told me he found an old, abandoned dock. It sounded like a creepy one, to be honest. It's already got a raggedy mobile home by it and some weird Catholic shrine, of all things. He said he's going to tear that stuff down and build an office for his business instead."

"A shrine?" My mind instantly flew to the baby-blue grotto Ruby kept next to her mobile home. How many of those things could there be out there on the bayou? "He's not talking about Ruby Oubre's land, is he?"

"I have no idea. He said he's already taken care of one problem, though." Sabine leaned forward, ready to give me more gossip. "Now he has to convince the next one in the family. I feel sorry for that person, whoever it is. You do *not* want to mess with my dad."

A shudder pinballed down my spine, and it had nothing to do with the air conditioner that had just clicked on. I'd seen Christophe d'Aulnay in the dining room at Miss Odilia's restaurant, when everyone parted to let him pass. He had the ability to silence an entire crowd without ever saying a word.

Before I could comment, though, she hopped from the bar stool and whisked the bookbag off the counter.

"Well, I'd better get going." She sounded giddy now, far different from when she first arrived. "I can't wait to see what you're going to come up with! I thought for sure you'd tell me to take a hike. See you later!"

With that, she twirled away from me and practically skipped to the front door. I waited long enough for her to pass through the exit before I whipped out my cell phone and tapped Lance's number at the Louisiana State Police Department on my speed dial.

At this rate, I didn't know what to tell Lance first. How I'd discovered an almost-empty bottle of Xanax in the mayor's office or how Captain d'Aulnay planned to take over Ruby's land.

Neither of the stories cast the men involved in a good light.

Chapter 22

I willed Lance to answer the telephone when the call went through, which he finally did on the fourth ring. "Hallelujah…you're there."

"Of course I'm here. I'm still working on the tip from Ruby Oubre's neighbor. Why? What's up?"

What isn't up? I wanted to say. First of all, I'd stumbled across a used pill bottle in the mayor's office. And not just any bottle…a prescription for Xanax, which just happened to be the medicine used to knock out Ruby before she drowned.

Plus, I had surprising news about Christophe d'Aulnay to consider. Not that he wanted Ruby's land—we all knew that—but how he needed it now to save his failing business.

Since I had to start with one topic, I chose Mayor Turcott because I had tangible evidence on that one.

"I found something in the mayor's office today, Lance. Something you should know about."

"First of all…what were you doing in his office?" He sounded peeved, as if he didn't approve of my wanderings.

"I had to go back to the Factory, and I noticed his car in the parking lot. Once I went upstairs, I found a used pill bottle in his trash can. It was a prescription for Xanax. Someone had crossed the patient's name out on the front."

"I have to be honest with you. I'm not sure it means anything. Think about it. Would you want people to know you were taking Xanax if you were the mayor?"

"No, I guess not."

"Most politicians have their assistants, or even their attorneys, have the prescription filled in their name. That way, a reporter can't get ahold of the information and use it against them."

"I'm sure it happens all the time. But, Lance—"

"It all started in the seventies." He spoke right over me. Luckily, we'd known each other long enough to know that neither of us would take offense when the other one interrupted. "I remember when my mom told me about it. She said some governor—I think it was the governor of Missouri—had to step down because people found out he'd been in a mental hospital. After that, politicians got real tricky about how they handled hospitalizations, medical tests...even prescriptions."

"You're talking about Governor Eagleton." Even I could hear the exasperation in my voice. "And I think it was the vice presidential ticket. But it doesn't matter. I'm trying to tell you something else. The pharmacist filled the bottle with thirty capsules on Wednesday. Now it looks like only three are left, at the most. Who takes that many Xanax in three days?"

The phone fell silent, and I could almost hear Lance's mind whirring. After an eternity, he came back on the call. "Normally, I'd agree with you. But there's something else you should know."

"What now?"

"I spoke to the mayor this morning because Hollis told me he came out to see his grandmother at the start of the week. The man has an airtight alibi for Thursday morning, when Ruby was killed."

"He does?"

"He was at a press conference to announce the opening of St. Bartholomew Health Center," Lance said. "His story checks out. KATZ covered it, plus a few other stations up in Baton Rouge."

"Oh." I tried not to sound disappointed, although I was sure Lance could read it in my voice.

"He got to the conference around six that morning. Apparently, radio reporters get to work extra early."

Now it was my turn to fall silent. I simply couldn't reconcile my hunch with what Lance had said. To be honest, the mayor seemed like the perfect suspect in Ruby's killing. He was arrogant; he was an outsider, since he hailed from Oklahoma, according to Hollis; and he was slick as anything. Too bad my jaded opinion of him didn't jibe with Lance's facts.

"Well, there's something else." I guessed it was time to revert to theory number two, which revolved around the d'Aulnay family and their dwindling fortune. "There's also Christophe d'Aulnay to consider. One of his daughters—Sabine—told me the family's going broke. Her father can't even pay for her wedding now."

"Hmmm," he said. "I'd heard tourism was down on the river."

"It's true. I don't know whether it's just affecting the d'Aulnay, or all the tour operators, but now Christophe d'Aulnay is scrambling for cash." It was hard to forget the desperation in Sabine's voice when she told me the news. "He wants to add another dock, and it looks like the dock he wants is Ruby's. Now, more than ever."

"I've spoken to him once, but only briefly. Think I'll pay him another visit today."

I glanced at the digital clock on my cash register, which read one. Since I'd left the bayou a while ago, I'd stranded Bo without a car and without any way to get lunch. "I need to head on back to Ruby's. I've got Ambrose's car, and he might need it. Let me know what you find out about Christophe d'Aulnay, okay?"

"Will do."

Once we said good-bye, I quickly extinguished the lights in the studio and headed out to the parking lot. Mayor Turcott's classic Thunderbird convertible was long gone by now.

Just as well. Since Mayor Turcott had an airtight alibi for Thursday morning, he wasn't a suspect in Ruby's killing anymore. Which meant it was time for me to focus on the real suspects, such as Christophe d'Aulnay.

By the time I arrived at the bayou, a headache niggled at the back of my brain…and that wasn't the worst part. A deep rumble also had wended its way through my stomach and settled just under my rib cage. If I didn't get some food soon, I'd surely faint.

I quickly pulled the car behind the dock and gingerly stepped out of it. After a few feet, though, I paused. Something was amiss, although I couldn't quite put my finger on it. Had I forgotten something?

One glance at the dock, and I had my answer. I forgot to bring more rawhide bones, so I was at Jacques's mercy, if he decided to surprise me again.

Head ducked and legs pumping, I hurried toward the staircase. In a flash, a low growl sounded behind me, which stopped me in my tracks.

This time it *wasn't* an airboat motor. Sure enough, as soon as I turned, I spied Jacques on the edge of the dock, his lips curled around something red and round and shiny. He seemed torn between wanting to ambush me and wanting to chew on his newfound toy.

"Ambrose? Hollis?" My voice sounded weak, compared to Jacques's growl. Plus, I didn't know if they'd even be inside the mobile home, since they might've walked somewhere.

"Anyone home?" Once more, my voice sounded squeaky. I quickly pondered my options. I could either wait for Jacques to make up his mind to pounce on me, or I could marshal my strength and call in the cavalry.

"Help!" This time, I screamed loudly.

The dog dropped the treasure on the dock and cocked his head in surprise.

Hallelujah, the ploy worked. The door to the mobile home banged open, and Ambrose flew down the stairs. He still carried the football, which he poised above his shoulder before he let the ball fly. I couldn't imagine what he had in mind, but at this point, I didn't care. As long as it kept Jacques away, I was on board.

"Hang tight," Ambrose said, as the ball sailed over our heads. It quickly spiraled toward the dog, where it glanced off its front paws.

Arrrrooo! The moment the dog stopped howling, he jumped off the dock and landed in the river with a splash.

Now *I* was the one to cock my head. "What was that all about?"

"Heck if I know," Bo said. "I just wanted to scare him off. I had no idea he'd head for the river. I didn't even know he could swim."

We watched Jacques dog-paddle toward shore, ribbons of water flying everywhere. He'd abandoned his treasure on the dock, and he seemed frantic to retrieve it.

"Of course he can swim. He's a water dog." It was Hollis, who had come up behind us.

I quickly turned. "What happened to you guys? I yelled your names, but no one answered. I thought I was all alone out here."

"We were messing around with the football on the other side of the house," Hollis said. "We went inside when we saw your car come up the road."

"Thank goodness. I thought I was a goner."

By the time I glanced over at Ambrose, he'd already stepped away from us. He'd begun to walk toward the dock, which seemed like a foolish thing to do, since Jacques could return at any moment. Why tempt fate again?

"Ambrose?" I tried to call him back, but he'd already arrived at the dock. Instead of reaching for the football, though, he lifted Jacques's red chew toy off the ground.

"What's that?" I asked Hollis, since Ambrose seemed preoccupied now.

"Beats me," Hollis said. "Looks like some trash Jacques found in the bushes. He likes to retrieve stuff and bring it back here."

We watched Ambrose gingerly appraise the object. First, he delicately turned it over in his palm, as if it might break, and then he held it up to the sun. It looked like a piece of plastic. Red plastic, with one end chewed off.

Once he finished studying it, Ambrose dropped his arm and returned to where we stood. "Look at this." He gingerly showed me his discovery.

I'd been right about the plastic. It was a used Solo cup, with the rim torn off in spots. Bits of the rim still clung to the cup, but barely.

"May I see that?" I asked.

Ambrose shrugged and handed it over. I gently took it from him, and then I quickly studied the cup's bottom, which Jacques had yet to gnaw.

"Just like I thought," I said, once I finished. "Someone put tomato juice in there."

"Huh?" Hollis pursed his lips. "We don't drink tomato juice. Gross. Maybe it came from the neighbor's trash."

"Maybe, but didn't you say your grandmother loved Bloody Marys? That's basically tomato juice and vodka."

Hollis didn't look convinced. "But she'd never use a cup like that. She had a special glass for her 'tonic.' Something she got in New Orleans one Mardi Gras.'"

I pointed the cup at Ambrose. "Here. Tell me what you think."

Sure enough, once Ambrose had a chance to study the cup, he nodded. "You're right. It looks like it used to be a Bloody Mary. That's dried tomato juice and some leftover celery."

"We need to give it to Lance for evidence," I said. "This could be the cup someone used to drug Ruby."

Considering the medical examiner had discovered alcohol in Ruby's bloodstream, along with the knockout drug, a Bloody Mary only made sense. The killer must've known that something strong, like vodka, could make the sedative work twice as fast. Not only that, but Hollis said it was Ruby's favorite drink, so she'd happily accept one if someone offered it to her.

Uh-oh. "I just thought of something else." Ambrose and Hollis gazed at me curiously, as they waited for the other shoe to drop. "Whoever killed Ruby knew her favorite drink. That means they weren't strangers."

The thought chilled me, and I fell silent. To think a friend, neighbor, or former employer even, could have killed Ruby was mind-boggling. Worst of all...who was to say they wouldn't kill again?

Chapter 23

We all studied the ground for a moment or two. Across from us, the dog sulked at the river's edge, mourning his lost toy. Every once in a while, he shot us a recriminating glance, as if he could guilt us into returning his treasure to the dock.

My stomach finally broke the silence with another—even louder—growl. "Heavens to Betsy." I'd been able to ignore the hunger pangs until now, but this was getting ridiculous.

"What was *that*?" Hollis asked.

"My stomach. I've hardly had anything to eat all day."

"We need to fix that." Ambrose took my hand and led me away from the dock.

I still held the crumpled Solo cup in my other hand, which I fully expected to give to Lance as soon as possible.

Before we got very far, though, someone's cell phone burst into song: "Gimme Three Steps."

I turned to Hollis, who was a huge Lynyrd Skynyrd fan, judging by his wardrobe.

He quickly reached into the pocket of his shorts and pulled out the ringing cell. "Hello?"

Ambrose smiled and leaned over to whisper in my ear, "Not a bad ringtone."

"True," I agreed, in an equally soft voice. "But he could've picked 'Free Bird.' That one has even better guitar riffs."

Before Ambrose could argue with me, Hollis turned away. He also stuck his index finger in his right ear, probably because he couldn't hear anything over our chatter.

"Where do you want to eat?" I whispered to Ambrose.

"Maybe some barbecue. That place on fourth street just reopened and I heard—"

"WHO IS THIS?" Hollis's voice boomed in the quiet.

I dropped Ambrose's hand and moved over to the teenager. "What's wrong?" I mouthed.

Hollis ignored me, though. "If you don't tell me who this is, I'm gonna hang up," he yelled into the phone.

"Don't do that," I hissed. "Lance needs to trace the call."

Finally, Hollis listened to me, and he even tilted the cell forward, so I could eavesdrop on the conversation.

The sound of static crackled over the line. Then a man's voice, or, more precisely, the hollow sound of someone speaking through a voice scrambler, filled the air.

"I can see you, you know," the wheezy voice said. "Get away from the house."

He sounded like Darth Vader breathing into his helmet. Either that, or a demon from the underworld trying to communicate with the living. A very angry demon from the underworld.

Hollis glanced at me helplessly, so I quickly spun my hands around—like a barrel rolling downhill—to signal he should keep talking. Fortunately, he caught on, and he brought the receiver back to his mouth.

"I'm...I'm sorry," he said. "But I can barely hear you. What's that you said?"

I braced for the wheezy voice to return, but the line had fallen silent. *Click.*

"Dagnabbit!" I said. "He must've realized what we were up to."

"Did I blow it?" Hollis looked mortified. "I'm sorry, but I didn't know what to say."

"That's okay. It's not your fault." No need to make him feel bad. Anyone would've panicked in the same situation. "I'll bet you Lance had enough time to trace it."

"Do you think so?"

"Sure." I had no idea how long Lance would need, and the call seemed incredibly short, to be honest. "It's amazing what those machines can pick up nowadays."

"She's right." Ambrose had moved over to us, and now we formed a tight circle. "The police have great technology now. I'll bet Lance can ID the location."

"But the guy sounded so mad." Hollis looked worried, and at least a dozen tiny wrinkles pleated his pale forehead now.

"Yes, he did sound mad," I said. "That's why we need to take the threat seriously. Let's get out of here for a while. I'll call Lance from the road."

Now that we had a plan, we walked back to Ambrose's car. I clicked the doors open with his fob, and then I handed the key ring back to Bo. Once I claimed the passenger seat, the red Solo cup still in my hand, Hollis hopped into the back and Ambrose slid behind the steering wheel.

I spied the dog from the corner of my eye as we pulled away from Ruby's property. He must've forgotten all about his earlier injury, because he padded toward the dock, aimlessly searching for the lost treasure.

"Where do you want to go?" Ambrose asked, once he'd driven us onto the surface road.

"As far away from the house as we can." Although I hated to admit it, the thought of someone watching us made my skin crawl.

The caller could be anywhere…behind that tree over there; beside that clump of kudzu; even within spitting distance of the cruiser driven by Lance's backup, which hadn't moved since this morning.

"Say, Ambrose." I craned my neck as we approached the police cruiser. "Can you please stop for a second? I want to talk to the police officer."

"No problem." He steered the Audi alongside the squad car. Once he lowered the driver's side window, I leaned over him to speak to the person in the other car.

"Hollis just got another phone call," I said. "Someone was using a voice scrambler again."

"I know." The policewoman, a pretty Hispanic with brown eyes and an ebony ponytail, nodded. "Lance just radioed to tell me about it. He's tracing the call now."

"Do we need to stick around?" I wanted her to say no, but there was no telling whether Lance would want us to stay put.

"No. It's okay if you leave. Once Lance gets the coordinates, he'll head over to the caller's location. Don't go too far, though. We'll need you to come to the station later."

"Gotcha. We won't go far."

With that, I leaned back in the passenger seat, raised the window, and felt the engine kick back into Drive. The scenery flowed by my window as we moved down the road. The kudzu reminded me of a lumpy green carpet someone had thrown over the tree branches. Bits of the river appeared when the foliage parted, and sun glanced off the water's surface.

"Anyone else get creeped out by that call?" I finally asked.

"Uh, yeah," Ambrose said. "No one wants to be watched."

When Hollis didn't answer, I turned to look at him. He sat with his chin on his chest, as if he was either thinking or he'd fallen fast asleep.

"Everything okay, Hollis?" I gently asked. I didn't want to wake him if he'd fallen asleep, but something told me he hadn't.

"Yeah, I'm fine." He lifted his head again. "I'm just glad you guys are with me. I don't know what I would've done if that guy had called when I was all alone."

"Good thing you don't have to worry about that. Let's hope Lance can trace the call."

I spun around and began to study the scenery again. Every once in a while, the hedge outside my window gave way to another view of the water and a stand of tupelos on the opposite shore. Soon the trees would shed their leaves, but for now they provided a webbed canopy of army-green leaves above the marshy ground.

After a minute or two, we passed an even larger gap in the brush. As we moved past it, I spied something strange, something totally unexpected. A boater had taken an airboat out on the river, and it kept pace with us on the water.

Not just any airboat, either. Painted black, the side bore the multicolored logo for BLEW-BY-YOU Boat Tours. It was hard to miss, since a giant alligator grinned at me from under a jaunty sailor's cap.

"Look…" My voice trailed off. There, in the driver's seat, perched high above the deck, sat Remy Gaudet. He was all alone in the boat, and every time he hit a rough patch, the empty seats below him bounced up and down. He steered the boat parallel to our car, but I couldn't hear the noise of the motor because of the air-conditioning vent in front of me.

All at once, I forgot where I was. Instead of the front seat of Ambrose's car, I found myself back in the parking lot at the Factory. Now my feet touched hard asphalt, instead of a carpeted floorboard. Across my lap, I felt my scratchy wool skirt, instead of the smooth nylon of Lululemon yoga pants.

I'd been in a hurry yesterday; that much I remembered. Lured by a gentle breeze and a few precious hours away from the shop. So preoccupied, I almost bumped into Remy Gaudet when we passed each other in the parking lot at the Factory.

He seemed antsy when I spoke to him. Almost eager to get away from me. Especially when I mentioned the bag in his hand.

It was a plastic bag from the Shoprite Deluxe. With a sticky note attached that read Suite 221. That was the mayor's address. Could the package have contained the leftover Xanax, which I'd found in the overturned trash can?

Someone had to use the medicine. Was it Remy Gaudet who spiked Ruby's drink and then made sure she ended up facedown in the river?

If so, why would he return an almost-empty pill bottle to the mayor's office? To get rid of it? Or to prove what he'd done, even though a police diver had found Ruby's body by then?

Come to think of it...maybe my theory wasn't so crazy, after all. Like wayward pieces of a jigsaw puzzle, I began to link one scene with another, even if they looked totally incompatible at first. It was an incomplete picture to start, but it solidified as I added more and more details.

For starters, Remy couldn't hear a thing without his hearing aids, and he wouldn't turn them up unless someone asked him to. Was that why a neighbor heard a commotion the morning Ruby was killed? Did Jacques sneak up on Remy? The dog could have ambushed him from behind since Remy couldn't hear the *click-clack* of canine toenails against hardwood planks.

Come to think of it, I'd noticed a limp when Remy walked away from me yesterday. Did Jacques take a bite out of the man's leg, which would make Remy holler even louder? A scream of surprise could travel for miles out here, with nothing to block it but a holey curtain of kudzu and some randomly spaced trees.

"What's wrong?" Ambrose's voice brought me back to the present. "You look like you've seen a ghost."

All at once, the soft breeze of the bayou changed to the cool flow of manufactured air as I returned to the front seat of the Audi. Instead of a wool skirt scratching my legs, I once more felt the slick nylon of yoga pants.

"Missy?"

"I haven't seen a ghost. Something worse. I think I know who killed Ruby."

Chapter 24

Hollis immediately reacted to the news. "Whoa! What did you say?" He lurched forward from the back seat of the car and squeezed into the space between Ambrose and me.

"I think Remy Gaudet killed your grandmother. And now he's following us. Look." I quickly pointed out the window, but we'd come to another thick patch of emerald kudzu and it blocked our view of the river.

"Are you sure?" Ambrose said. "I don't see anything." He cut his gaze from the road to the river, but only for an instant. "That sounds kinda crazy, Missy."

"Just watch." I waited until the car moved past the hedge and another gap appeared. "There. Look now."

Sure enough, once the kudzu parted, we had a clear shot of Remy and his airboat. And while we studied *him,* he watched *us* through a pair of oversized binoculars, which he held in one hand while he grasped the boat's steering mechanism with the other.

"What's he doing out there?" Hollis spat the words, clearly incensed.

"I think he wants to stop us," I said. "He's probably afraid we figured everything out."

The minute I said that, though, I paused. *Is it really possible?* Did Remy Gaudet kill Ruby and then make threatening phone calls to Hollis from his business? Maybe he thought we'd stumbled across the truth and now we were headed for the police station to alert Lance. We couldn't simply call Lance with a cell, not with the iffy phone service out here, so maybe he worried we were on our way to the police station to deliver the news in person.

Is that why he was following us...to stop us, before it was too late?

"I still think it's far-fetched," Ambrose said. "Isn't it?"

"Maybe, but maybe not," I answered. "Maybe he knows we figured it out. And he wants to make sure we don't tell anyone else."

"I still don't get it, Miss DuBois." Hollis sat so close, his breath tickled my ear. "How do you know for sure he killed my grandma?"

"Because he's the one who got the medicine from the pharmacy. And somehow all those pills disappeared in three days. Plus, he's practically deaf without his hearing aids, and I think that's why Jacques was able to surprise him on the dock. Look...you can see for yourself he's trying to flag us down."

One glance out the window confirmed it. Instead of watching us through the binoculars, now Remy waved them at us, as if he wanted us to pull over and meet with him.

Fat chance of that.

"But *why* would he do it?" Hollis still sounded incredulous, and incredibly angry.

"For your property, of course. He thought he'd go about it the right way and present your grandmother with that letter of intent. But when she ignored it, he got so mad he probably couldn't see straight. That's when he must've decided to get rid of her."

Only one piece of the puzzle remained, something that had bothered me from the start. "Now I need to figure out how Remy scraped together enough money to make a real estate offer. Lance told me all the swamp tour operators out here are suffering. Since he brought the used prescription bottle to the mayor's office, maybe it was the mayor who gave it to him."

"Whoa. Hold on." Once more, Ambrose shifted his gaze from the road to the river, but only for a second. "Now you're talking crazy. You think the mayor's involved in this?"

Before I could answer him, though, our car skidded to a stop. We'd reached a fork in the road, and both paths looked promising.

"I forgot the best way to get out of here," Ambrose said.

"Beats me." I gave him a half-hearted shrug. "I don't know the roads out here."

Unlike Ambrose and me, though, Hollis didn't hesitate. "Go right."

Ambrose jerked the steering wheel right, and we bumped onto a different, thinner surface road that took us along the river.

"We'll go down here for about a half mile." Hollis barked the directions from his spot between us. "The road's kinda rough, but it's the best way."

I was about to ask him, "the way to what?" but I didn't bother. I was too busy searching for another hole in the kudzu so I could keep my eye on Remy.

Unfortunately, the hedge grew thick and tall here. I rolled down the passenger window to see whether I could hear the airboat engine, and soon the buzz of spinning metal reached me. The fan blades sounded like a giant cicada that'd landed on the roof of our car and decided to stay there.

"Turn left here." It was Hollis again, his voice as firm as before.

I closed the passenger window and withdrew my cell phone from my pocket. "I definitely need to call Lance. Maybe I'll finally get a good connection."

It took a second for the call to link me with Lance's cell, once I pressed the number on my speed dial. The moment it went through, though, Lance answered it.

"Hiya, Missy. I was just about—"

"No time, Lance. I think I know who killed Ruby."

While I didn't relish the thought of rehashing everything in front of Hollis again—he already sounded livid—it couldn't be helped. So, I quickly told Lance all about the package from the Shoprite Deluxe, the way Jacques must've attacked Remy on the dock, and how Remy had jumped into his airboat to follow us once we left the property.

The moment I finished, Lance gave a long, low whistle. "That sounds about right. We got a positive ID on the phone call just now. It came from Remy's landline...the one licensed to BLEW-BY-YOU Boat Tours."

"I knew it!" While I didn't enjoy being right—who would've thought the elderly swamp boat captain was capable of murdering Ruby—it felt good to know I wasn't grasping at straws. Speaking of which...

"There's more, Lance. I think the mayor could be involved."

"The mayor? Hold on a sec. I need to turn on my siren."

After a moment, the high-pitched whine of a police siren sounded over the other end of the phone.

"You're already in your car?" I asked.

"Of course. The minute I found out who made the phone call, I left headquarters. I'll be at Remy's boat slip in a few minutes."

I placed my palm over the phone so I could speak with Ambrose. "Lance knows it was Remy who killed her, and he's headed out here."

"Missy!" Lance's voice sounded through the gaps in my fingers.

"Sorry, Lance." I quickly removed my hand. "I wanted to tell Ambrose what's going on."

"Now, repeat what you just said. You think the mayor's involved?"

"I do. Remember the prescription bottle I found in Mayor Turcott's office? Why would Remy return the bottle there unless the mayor was in on it? Maybe they thought no one would ever check the mayor's trash, but they weren't too sure about Remy's property."

"I get that," Lance said. The staccato sound of a siren in the background underscored his words. "But why would the mayor help out Remy? What did he have to gain?"

"You said the tour operators around here were having a hard time. But Zephirin Turcott is loaded with cash. Just look at the man's clothes and that fancy car. And he's smart. He's probably charging Remy an arm and a leg to loan him the money. I know for a fact the guy doesn't have any morals. He proved it when he gave Antonella Goode a pass on the building code just because her parents helped fund his election campaign."

"Hold on a sec," Lance said. "I have to process everything. Okay, then. Here's the deal." He'd hardened his voice, which gave me a sneaky suspicion of what he was about to say next. "I don't want you going anywhere near Remy's property right now. I'm serious this time."

"What makes you think—"

"Save it, Missy. I know you. Please stay away from it."

Before I could defend myself, he hung up.

"Of all the nerve!" I reluctantly lowered my cell phone. "He hung up on me. Can you believe it?"

"Actually," Ambrose said, "I *can* believe it. At some point, you're going to have to back off from these police investigations. No one wants you to get hurt."

"I have no idea what you're talking about." I tried to sound sincere, although I knew *exactly* what he was talking about.

It all started a few years ago, when I first moved to Bleu Bayou. Somehow, I developed a strange knack for figuring out who killed the victims in a series of high-profile crimes. Now Lance called me whenever he had an unsolved crime and a passel of likely suspects. Was it my fault I'd discovered a hidden talent? It was one I didn't ask for, and I'd certainly love to be free of it.

"...police do their job." Apparently, Ambrose was still talking, so I pretended I'd been listening all along.

"Um-hmmm," I murmured. "But it's not my fault I happen to be in the thick of things whenever criminals get caught. You know Lance sometimes acts like I'm his pesky kid sister. Like I purposefully try to insert myself into these cases, which couldn't be further from the truth."

"Uh, Missy?"

Something in Ambrose's voice made me shut up. He was staring out the windshield, so I followed his gaze to see what was so intriguing.

We'd come to another bend in the road, only this one didn't have any shrubs or trees or kudzu to block the view. This time, a building stood front and center on the shoreline. A weathered wood building with a corrugated tin roof and a battered neon sign. I watched Remy angle his airboat toward the property and gun the motor, as he headed straight for the property's timeworn dock.

Meanwhile, Ambrose cut his eyes to the rearview mirror. "Hollis, what've you done? This isn't a backdoor way to the police station."

"I…I…" Hollis slowly pulled away from the front seat, as if he wanted to put as much distance as possible between him and Ambrose.

I finally realized what they were talking about. The fluorescent letters in the neon sign spelled out BLEW-BY-YOU Boat Tours, which was clearly visible, even in daylight.

"Hollis," I said. "Why did you bring us here?"

"Because he's guilty! You said so yourself." Although he'd pulled away from the front seat, his voice came through loud and clear. "I don't want him to get away with it."

"No one's getting away with anything." I spoke gently, but firmly. "Lance will be here in a second. He needs to be the one to take Remy into custody. Not you, and not me."

By now, Remy's airboat had reached the dock. Once he pulled alongside the planks, he scrambled off the sky-high seat and quickly tossed a length of rope over the side of the boat. The cord caught around one of a half-dozen cleats soldered to the planks, and the boat jerked to a stop.

"What does he think he's doing?" I watched him head for the wood shack, my heartbeat quickening in my chest.

Thankfully, I didn't have to wonder for long. At that moment, a white police cruiser skidded onto the riverbank, its lights flashing and siren wailing. The pretty Latino policewoman from before jumped out of the car when it stopped, and then she trained her Glock on Remy, who instantly froze.

"Look!" I said. "Lance must've radioed his backup."

We all watched Remy slowly lift his arms to the sky. He held them there until the policewoman reached his side and slapped a pair of glossy handcuffs around his wrists. Then, she pushed him forward, and he began to walk stiff-legged to the edge of the dock.

"Let's go down there, Bo," I said. "It's okay now."

Thankfully, he agreed with me, and he quickly shifted the Audi back into Drive. By the time we arrived at the dock, we were joined by Lance, who zoomed onto the property in his mud-splattered Buick Oldsmobile. A temporary light bar on the Buick's roof cast candy-cane swirls of red and white against the inky black of the airboat.

"Lance!" I shouted, as soon as the car stopped, and it was safe to jump outside.

My friend met me by the hood of his Buick, and then we headed for the dock, where the policewoman was reading Remy his Miranda rights.

To look at the swamp boat captain now, it was hard to imagine I'd ever been afraid of the man. That first time on Ruby's dock, when he'd brandished a heavy metal flashlight overhead, I thought he could use it against Hollis, and that frightened me.

Now, though, his head lolled against his chest, and his shoulders sagged forward miserably. He only glanced up when he heard Lance and me approach, and then he quickly straightened.

"I'm not da one ya want," he snapped.

The policewoman tried to silence him, but he ignored her.

"Ya tink I done all dis by myself?"

"Time to start talking, then." Lance gave a casual shrug, as if he had all the time in the world to hear Remy out.

"It's da mayor ya want, not me," Remy said.

"Of course it is. We knew that all along." Lance was bluffing, since we didn't know for sure the mayor was involved, but Remy didn't know that. "Tell me something I don't know."

"It was Turcott's idea." Remy spat the words, as if he couldn't spew them out fast enough. "He gave me a hundred grand cash money. Said it'd be easy. Said no one would ever care about an ol' lady."

"Why, you—" Hollis spun out from behind Lance.

I had no idea he'd even left Ambrose's car, let alone followed us to the dock. The moment he shot past us, though, Lance lurched forward and grabbed him by the arms.

"Not so fast." Lance pinned the teen's arms to his sides. "Walk away from him, Hollis. He's not worth it."

Hollis couldn't, or wouldn't, listen to him. He continued to struggle, his eyes wild. "He can't get away with this. And he can't say that about Grandma. Of course, people care. Let...me...go."

"No way." Unlike Hollis, Lance sounded completely calm. He held the teen for several seconds, until the boy's body gradually went limp. "There. That's better."

In the meantime, Ambrose had headed for the dock too, and he slung his arm around my shoulders the moment he reached me. "Are you okay?" Worry clouded his face.

"Yes." I nodded, finally able to catch my breath again. "I'm fine."

The policewoman marched Remy to her cruiser, and then she dipped his head low to maneuver him into the back seat. Once she slammed the passenger door shut, she walked over to the driver's side.

"I really didn't want to be right," I said, to no one in particular.

The police lights threw shafts of red and white against the greenery as the cruiser pulled away.

"But I knew it had to be Remy."

Ambrose nodded. "And don't forget about the mayor. Sounds like they were both to blame."

"What's next, Lance?" I asked.

He stood beside Hollis, with his arms around the teen. The struggle seemed to have knocked the wind out of both of them. "Whew," he said. "Guess it's time to pay a visit to our illustrious mayor."

"That's what I thought you'd say." I knew the routine by now, and I knew the next step would be to take Mayor Turcott into custody.

"'Course...I could use some help." Lance grinned, even though he was breathing hard. "You know your way around the Factory better than anyone. And I'm guessing that's where we'll find the mayor."

"Are you asking me to go with you?" While I normally wouldn't hesitate, I was surprised to hear that, since our last phone call didn't go so well.

"It depends. Are you offering to help?"

"Maybe." I glanced at Ambrose, who waited patiently beside me. "As long as my fiancé doesn't mind."

"I don't think I could stop you if I tried," Ambrose said. "Go get 'im, Missy."

Chapter 25

Now that I had Ambrose's blessing, the bayou didn't seem nearly as ominous as we cruised along a back road in Lance's Oldsmobile.

Of course, I had to sweep aside an empty Doritos bag before I could plant my feet on the floorboard, and a week's worth of old Diet Coke cans rattled around in the back seat, but that was par for the course. I even stashed the red Solo cup in the glove compartment, once I told Lance about the find, so it wouldn't get lost with the other trash.

But, all in all, there was nowhere else I'd rather be.

To think Mayor Zephirin Turcott had waltzed into Bleu Bayou maybe six months before his election, if my hunch was correct, was inconceivable. He obviously didn't care about the people who lived in our town. If he did, he would've tried to protect someone like Ruby, instead of helping orchestrate her death.

And what about the money he accepted from the Goode family? Although I didn't know how much the Louisiana legislature allowed people to donate to a mayor's campaign, I suspected he accepted much more than the law allowed. Maybe I'd contact the state's attorney general's office after everything was said and done because they'd, no doubt, want to know about it.

"Lemme see if I've got this straight." Lance navigated the Buick down Highway 18. "Remy delivered a package to the mayor's office and it held the used prescription bottle. A prescription for Xanax."

I nodded distractedly. Now, instead of seeing the Atchafalaya River beyond my window, I spied one sugarcane field after another as we drove along, the stalks fat and ripe for the fall harvest. We'd soon approach the

Marathon Oil refinery, which culled its oil from the river's depths, and after that would come Bleu Bayou.

"Yep. Remy and the mayor must've struck a deal. Once Remy knocked out Ruby with the medicine and pushed her into the river, he was supposed to take the evidence back to the mayor's office. I'm not surprised…Mayor Turcott strikes me as arrogant enough to think no one would ever suspect him of being involved."

"They almost got away with it too," Lance said. "Without an eyewitness, it would've been hard to prove who was behind Ruby's death. The medical examiner could confirm the alcohol and drugs, but none of us knew who gave them to her. Unfortunately, they don't have security cameras out on the bayou."

"Thank God for that." When Lance threw me a funny look, I quickly spoke again. "Would you really want them there? I don't think technology will ever replace plain-old conversation. It was Miss Lucy's tip that helped us crack the case."

"True, but sometimes people down here trade in gossip instead of news."

"That's because there's not a whole lot of difference. My point is you don't need high-tech gadgets when you've got neighbors to watch out for you."

"Amen to that," he said. "And did you notice how fast Remy ratted out the mayor? He couldn't wait to turn on him."

"Guess he never had enough money to buy Ruby's land after all. I wonder what kind of interest rate Turcott was charging him? Something astronomical, of course."

"By the way, I called the circuit judge while you were talking to Ambrose. He ordered an emergency search warrant for the mayor's office."

"Good." Our drive had finally taken us past the refinery, which blazed against the midafternoon sky. Sunlight bounced off its silvered sides, like a shiny jungle gym on a child's playground.

"I just hope the mayor's in his office," Lance said.

"He will be. He's spearheading a grand-opening party for Antonella Goode's store. He told me he still had a ton of details to work out."

"You mentioned something about that girl before. Who is she, and why's she so important to you?"

"She's not important to me." I spoke quickly, before I could change my mind. To be honest, I'd probably given my competitor way too much thought, given everything else that'd happened over the last few days. Maybe it was time to let Antonella's store thrive or fail on its own, without any interference from me. I might not like it, but I'd come to realize there was precious little I could—or should—do about it.

"Okay…maybe she's a little important to me. But mainly because she's the reason I got to see the mayor's true colors. I foolishly went to him when I found out Antonella was breaking the law, but the Goode family supported his election campaign, and he wasn't about to mess with one of their daughters."

"Gotcha. Are you ready to do this, then?" He nodded toward the windshield, where the outline of the Factory appeared. Like always, the two-story building soared above its neighbors, with a saw-toothed roofline that rose and dipped against the horizon.

"I am. I'll let you take him into custody, but I can't wait to see what he has to say for himself."

The parking lot was nearly empty when we arrived. Since the afternoon was half over, even the Saturday appointments had gone home. But, hallelujah, the mayor's powder-blue Thunderbird sat front and center in the first row, with its convertible top down and its rich leather upholstery exposed to the elements.

Lance pulled up next to the T-bird and gingerly stepped from the car. I did the same, before I joined him on the sidewalk and we headed for the building's lobby.

Our footfalls sounded hollow once we entered the glass pyramid and trekked across its marble floor. After riding the elevator to the second floor, we exited the car and made our way down the long hall.

For some reason, the air seemed thinner by the time we reached the last crate label, and I had trouble catching my breath. It wasn't exactly the thought of apprehending the mayor that frightened me. After all, the man had nothing to gain, and everything to lose, by resisting arrest. No, the problem lay in not knowing. Sometimes people reacted exactly as you expected, while other times they behaved completely out of character. Those were the times when anything could happen and nothing was a sure bet. Mayor Turcott might surprise us yet, and that was what made it hard to breathe.

"What are we going to do first, Lance?" I asked, as we approached the mayor's office. By now, the sun had traveled westward, to the other side of the building, which left the beige walls looking muddy from the weak light that shone through a few windows.

"If I'm remembering right, there's a front lobby when you get through the door to the mayor's office."

I nodded. "You're right. A receptionist usually sits behind a desk there. But not on weekends." It seemed a lifetime had passed since I'd last entered this door, and not just a few hours. "Once you get inside, look for another door near the bookcase. That'll lead you to the mayor's personal office, which is on the left."

"See? This is why I take you places."

"Very funny. I thought it was because of my sparkling personality." I couldn't resist the urge to tease him, even though tension electrified the air.

"I want you to stay in the front area. Let me go into the mayor's office by myself."

"Gotcha. Just so you know...there's also a washroom next door. If he's not behind his desk, he's probably there."

"Okay." Slowly, Lance withdrew a Glock 22 from the waistband of his slacks and moved to the door. The knob turned freely, like before, and he quietly slipped into the office, with me on his heels.

The overheads cast yellow light across the room, which dulled the varnish on the mahogany furniture. I cautiously perched on the edge of a straight-backed chair, while Lance approached the inner door. Before he could turn the knob on that one, though, it swung open and Mayor Turcott burst into the anteroom.

"What the...?" He looked as surprised as I felt.

Lance didn't hesitate, though. He leveled his gun at the mayor with a steady hand. "You need to come with me."

The man blinked, but he didn't back away. "You're kidding, right? On what grounds?" His gaze ping-ponged around the room, until it landed on me. "Miss DuBois? What's going on?"

"You're wanted in the murder of Ruby Oubre," Lance spoke on my behalf, and he sounded surprisingly calm. As if he did this kind of thing every day, and he'd probably do it all again tomorrow.

"Murder? What the devil are you talking about?" The mayor's tone was condescending, as if Lance's words were pesky houseflies he could somehow shoo away with a flick of his wrist.

"We know you were behind the murder of Ruby Oubre," Lance repeated. "We talked to Remy Gaudet a few minutes ago."

"Remy?" At the mention of the swamp boat captain's name, the mayor's demeanor changed once again. Now he tried to laugh, but it was too shrill to be real. "The guy that runs swamp tours? You know he's crazy, right?" He leaned forward conspiratorially, as if he was going to let us in on a little secret. "He might be a little touched in the head. Probably has sunstroke from all those hours on the river."

"Nice try." Lance reached for a pair of handcuffs stuffed into the other side of his waistband. "You have the right to remain silent—"

At that moment, something loud banged into the wall next to us. *Cccrrrasshhh!*

The mayor recovered first, and he lurched back, retreating through the doorway to his inner office. Lance was only a heartbeat behind him, though, and he lifted the Glock to fire a single warning shot at the ceiling. Bits of fiberboard rained down on us, and I automatically covered my head with my arms.

Everything slowed at that point. After the shot, the mayor once again froze, openmouthed, in the doorway to where his office lay. Lance plunged forward and grabbed the man's wrists. An instant later, with a flash of silver and the click of a lock engaging, the two men stood face-to-face, with Turcott safely bound in a pair of handcuffs.

"This...this is an outrage!" the mayor huffed, apparently grasping at straws now. "I already told you where I was Thursday morning. It was all over the news. Are you stupid?"

Lance didn't bother to respond. Instead, he took up the Miranda rights again, exactly where he'd left off. "Anything you say can and will be used against you in a court of law."

"Miss DuBois?" The mayor looked at me with drowning eyes now, as if I was his last hope. "Say something."

"Fine," I said. "You're wanted for the murder of Ruby Oubre."

He glared at me angrily. Thank goodness for the handcuffs and Lance's firm grasp on his arm.

By the time we were ready to leave, the last of the splintered ceiling tiles had floated to the ground, and Lance pushed the shackled man toward the doorway. I slowly rose from my perch and joined them, eager to put the scene behind me. While an ordinary person would've realized he didn't stand a chance in this situation, the mayor was anything but ordinary. He thrust out his chin and marched toward the elevator as if he expected a welcome parade when the doors whisked open.

The arrogance was overwhelming. Either that, or he was a wonderful actor. Which sparked another thought as I followed the two men into the empty elevator car.

"I just thought of something." I tried to focus on Lance, since I didn't want the mayor to intimidate me, but I couldn't help watching him from the corner of my eye. "What if Mayor Turcott here has a police record back in Oklahoma?"

Sure enough, the mayor blinked. Just once, but it was enough to convince me I was right.

"I mean, how much did we really know about him before the election?" I asked.

"That's preposterous." Out came the mayor's condescending tone, which I'd expected. "Now you're the one who sounds stupid."

"That's not a bad hunch, Missy." Lance punched a button to send the elevator down one floor. "And it'll be easy enough to prove, once we get back to the station. There's no telling what our boy here has done." He jerked his head to indicate the mayor, who'd abruptly fallen silent. Apparently, the man who'd fooled an entire town couldn't even remember his next line.

"Cat got your tongue?" Lance asked.

"I'm warning you," the mayor said. "Let me go or my lawyer will eat you alive. You'll be sorry you ever started this."

Slowly, the elevator door creaked open to expose the empty lobby.

"Don't count on it," I said. "Lance here is four for four when it comes to putting murderers behind bars. Once he starts on something, he always finishes it."

Epilogue

The pirogue sluiced through the calm waters of the Atchafalaya, the soft *whhhiiirrr* of the outboard motor accompanied by the caw of a spoonbill overhead.

This time, it wasn't my assistant who manned the tiller, but Ambrose, who'd bundled up against the late-spring cold in a Columbia jacket and faded blue jeans.

He carefully steered the pirogue around clumps of floating hydrilla, lily pads the size of throw pillows, and knobby tupelo roots that dimpled the water.

"We're almost there," I said. "It's just past that big stump."

A lot had happened since my last trip down the river. For one thing, a jury of his peers had found Remy Gaudet guilty of first-degree murder, given the crime was willful and carefully orchestrated.

For his part, Zephirin Turcott received a life sentence for solicitation, since he'd put Remy up to the crime. Both of those rulings stashed the men behind bars for good, which no one mourned. Other than the defendants, of course.

My hunch about Zephirin Turcott's criminal record? Easy enough to prove once Lance connected with the Oklahoma City Police Department on Colcord Drive. The man had a rap sheet several pages long, and his "record of arrests and prosecutions" was well-known in that city's police department.

The record mostly consisted of petty larceny, since Zephirin had a fondness for separating wealthy widows from their Tiffany jewelry, but he also faced another solicitation charge when he bribed a Jiffy Lube mechanic to jackknife his ex-wife's Mercedes. Too bad that charge was dropped because it could've alerted the *Bleu Bayou Impartial Reporter* to the man's criminal record and quashed his bid for mayor.

"Did you see that one?" Ambrose pointed out a pink spoonbill, just like the one I'd admired on my earlier journey.

"Pretty, isn't it? The birds around here eat shrimp that turns them pink."

"Listen to you." He laughed. "Three years down South and you're already sounding like a local."

To be honest, I couldn't wait to come back to the river. Once the dust settled with the criminal trials and whatnot, it was the first thing I wanted to do. Especially after I got a phone call from Hollis, which happened about a week ago.

He called me on a Saturday morning, just as I was settling into a backyard swing to survey my pretty birdhouse. A kiskadee shyly approached the quarter-sized opening that led inside the birdhouse when...*bbbrrriiinnnggg!*

"Hello?" I didn't even bother to answer with my name this time, since the call had interrupted a perfectly good reverie.

"Is that you, Miss DuBois? It's me...Hollis."

"Hollis! So good to hear from you!" I hopped from the swing and walked a bit closer to the live oak. What with the early hour, my breath fogged the air as I spoke. "What've you been up to?"

"This 'n' that," he said, in that casual way of his. "I have a surprise for you."

"A surprise?" I squinted at the cell phone. "What kind of surprise?"

"I'm not telling you until you get here. Can you come to my grandma's property?"

"I suppose." The kiskadee shyly approached the strange opening, but it seemed more confused than anything. "Sure, I'll come out and see you. I haven't been out there since, you know..."

"I know. And thanks for letting me stay with you guys for so long."

Once Ruby's funeral passed and assorted Oubre relatives paid their respects, including Ruby's sister, whom Hollis tracked down with the help of the Internet, Ambrose and I invited him to come live with us.

He reluctantly obliged, since he didn't relish the thought of returning to his grandmother's property, where he'd received those eerie, threatening phone calls. Who could blame him for wanting to distance himself from the bayou, after everything that had happened there?

And once he moved in with us, Hollis blended into our household with no problem. In addition to being a crack handyman, which was something I appreciated since Ambrose didn't possess that particular skill, Hollis proved to be a natural businessman.

He took the lesson I gave him about marketing to heart. That initial lesson at his grandmother's kitchen table sparked a love for the subject that resulted in several online classes from a local community college. Afterward, he upgraded my website at Crowning Glory, and he performed some complicated Internet hacks that saved me time and money when it came to promoting my business. All in all, I loved spending time with the teenager, and I teared up the day he returned to his grandmother's homestead. We continued to chitchat about the shop, his classes, and whatnot until it was time to end our phone call.

"By the way, could you ask Mr. Jackson to come too? I'd like him to be here when I show you my surprise."

"Now I'm really curious. Can't you give me a hint?"

He hemmed and hawed a bit, so I decided to put him out of his misery.

"That's okay. You don't have to tell me. We'll come down next weekend. And we can't wait to see what you've done with the place."

Contrary to Christophe d'Aulnay's opinion, Hollis was quite capable of tending to his grandmother's property, thank you very much. I'd worried about it until Hollis had assured me he could handle anything the old house, and the Atchafalaya, had to throw at him. He sounded just like his grandmother when he said that, which told me he was going to be alright.

Once I hung up from our call, and the kiskadee flew away for good, I raced inside to tell Ambrose the news. Neither of us had any idea what the surprise could be, and we both looked forward to finding out.

That was how we found ourselves in Hank Dupre's pirogue, navigating the Atchafalaya on a crisp Saturday morning, with a spoonbill overhead and gnarled tupelo roots underneath.

Ambrose slowly guided the pirogue around the huge tree stump until the boat's stern cleared the knobby wood. I tried to stand, since I was so excited to see Hollis, but the swaying underfoot convinced me to stay put.

Sure enough, once we rounded the bend, the plot of land Ruby had called home for forty years came into view.

What a difference! Instead of a beige mobile home limned with mold, and a rickety boat dock on the verge of collapse, I spied a freshly painted single-wide with a sturdy aluminum dock. The house was beautiful... edged with river rocks and painted pewter. Hollis had replaced the flat roof with an A-line version, so now rainwater could slide down the sides instead of puddling in the middle. He also replaced the asphalt top with corrugated tin, which made the house look like one of those fancy "rustic retreats" producers like to feature on home design shows.

The dock looked amazing too, with two stories that included a viewing deck on top and a boat ramp down below. Everything was brand new, except for a baby-blue rock grotto next to the house.

Apparently, Hollis couldn't part with his grandmother's shrine to the Virgin Mary. Which was fine by me, since it probably protected Hollis when Remy came gunning for him all those months ago.

Best of all, a vinyl banner over the dock proclaimed: CAJUN COUNTRY ALLIGATOR FARM.

"Look at that, Ambrose!"

Only then did I notice a sturdy chain-link fence that cut the dock in half. One side of it allowed boats, like ours, to tie up to a cleat, while the other side protected some alligators that lounged on the shoreline.

Even Jacques participated in the new business, since the dog guarded the fence as if he wanted to protect "his" pets. He nosed the air when our boat drew close, but he didn't crouch on all fours this time.

"I can't believe Hollis actually started an alligator farm," I said.

At that moment, a figure appeared on the mobile home's deck. It was Hollis, wearing a Lynyrd Skynyrd T-shirt, of course, but he'd added a pair of waders instead of the Nike shorts. He began to wave at us the moment he saw the boat, and he didn't stop until our pirogue pulled alongside the dock.

"You came!" Hollis bounded down to the shore to meet us.

"I promised we would." When Hollis offered me his hand, I placed my palm in his. At the last minute, I remembered something, and my face fell.

"Uh-oh. I forgot to bring a treat for Jacques. Think he'll remember me?"

Hollis laughed. "You don't have to worry about him anymore. I finally figured out his breed. He's a cattle dog, only now he thinks he needs to herd the alligators. All he ever wanted was a job, I guess."

Sure enough, Jacques finally sat up, but he didn't lunge forward. Instead, he glanced back to make sure his charges were safe, and then he calmly sat down again.

"I'll be darned. Who would've thought that's all he ever wanted?" I hoisted myself onto the dock with Hollis's help, and then I turned to offer Ambrose a hand.

Once we both stood on the aluminum planks, Hollis indicated the baby-blue rock grotto next to the house. "See? I kept it there for Grandma. She would've wanted me to."

"You're right," I said. "And I hope you visit it sometimes."

"Not just me," Hollis said. "Everyone comes around to visit it now. I've had people leave behind pictures, notes...you name it. It's kind of a big deal."

This time, it was my turn to smile. "That's lovely. And now we have some news for *you*." I reached for Ambrose's hand, which he gladly gave me. "We've set a date for our wedding."

"Alright!" Hollis's face lit up. "It's about time you two got married. When'll it be?"

"August tenth. We're going to get married on the *Riverboat Queen*."

"That's awesome," Hollis said. "The captain sure changed his tune after everything happened with Grandma. He got nice, all of a sudden. He even came down here to help me get the dock ready for customers. That's his lettering on the sign."

"And I worked out a trade with him," I said. "I made a veil for his daughter's wedding, so he's letting us use the *Riverboat Queen* as a thank-you. It'll be a Southern wedding, with some zydeco and all the shrimp and grits you can eat."

Ambrose rustled next to me, trying to get a word in edgewise, I suppose. "I'd like you to be my best man, Hollis."

"I'd be honored, sir."

The moment he said that, Jacques gave a happy bark. Sometimes, things really did work out in the end.

Made in the USA
Coppell, TX
28 May 2020

26615228R00100